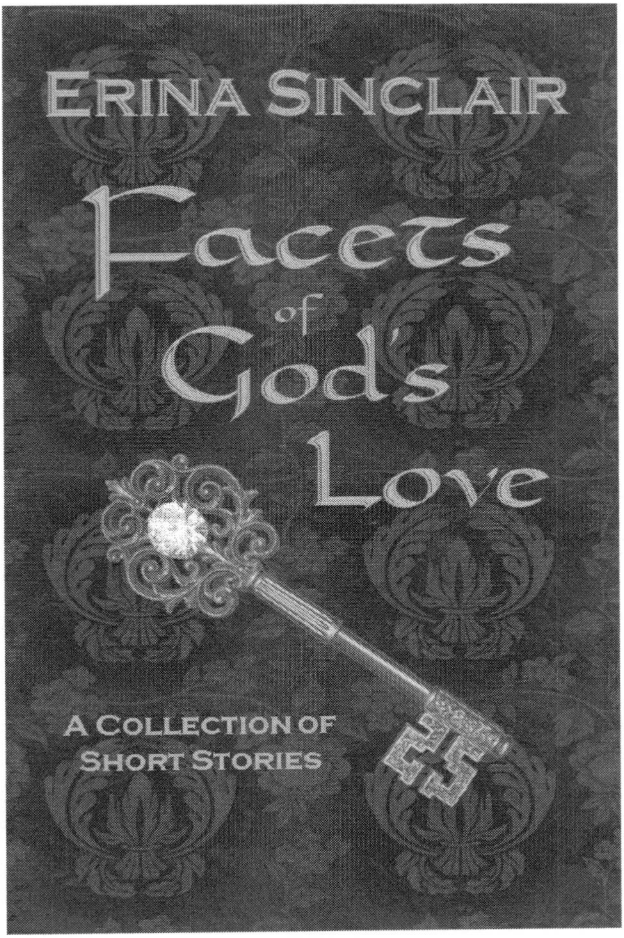
ERINA SINCLAIR
Facets
of
God's
Love
A COLLECTION OF
SHORT STORIES

Paperback ISBN-13: 978-1-948026-99-4
Digital ISBN-13: 978-1-948026-98-7

Scripture quotations are from The Holy Bible, King James Version, public domain.

Published by TMP Books, 3 Central Plaza Ste 307, Rome, GA 30161

www.TMPBooks.com

Published in the United States of America.

DEDICATION

"Commit Thy Work to God"

To God, my Father

Romans 8:14-15

"For as many as are led by the Spirit of God,

they are the sons of God.

For ye have not received the spirit of bondage again to fear;

but ye have received the Spirit of adoption, whereby we cry,

Abba, Father."

ACKNOWLEDGEMENTS

For my Blonde Boy. I love you.

For Pastors Jerry and Jeremy, thank you for your help and guidance.

For all the women who have "adopted" me throughout my lifetime, you are an inspiration and comfort to me, now and always.

CONTENTS

SPARED

God's Love Delivers

ONE

"Stand!" Nama commanded the figure before him. He swept a long, swarthy arm around the practice ground and walkway leading from the sands to the entrance. Six guards lay dead. Two more flanked him, sides heaving and sweaty, eyes thirsty for blood. "I think you've made your point."

The culprit crouched low in a fighting stance, fists up, feet planted wide, back facing the stone wall of the gladiatorial training ground. He bared his teeth and hissed like a wild animal, tossing his black, filth-matted locks over his bare, tattooed shoulders.

Nama sneered. The little rodent actually thought victory was possible even though he swayed from blood loss. He favored the idiot with a sardonic smile. The crouched figure rocked forward with a rasping gurgle, his eyes rolling back in his head as he collapsed in a heap. Behind him huddled the trembling form of a young woman. As she darted forward to help her companion, Nama waved his guards back. He swept the little figure with a harsh glare.

The woman stood slowly and faced him without a word or a twitch. Her gray eyes made their way up his frame as he stood with his arms folded across his chest and his huge hands balled into fists. Finally, she met his eyes. He returned her gaze with all the ferocity of his training as a gladiator. She trembled ever so slightly under his glare.

"Please," she quavered. "Spare him."

The sneer evaporated from Nama's face. He arched his eyebrow. *Swahili*? He cocked his head. How did she know his mother-tongue? Why did she not beg or cry or plead? Why the simple everyday request? A request so preposterous that he almost laughed aloud. But Swahili?

"Spare whom?" he addressed the woman in kind as if he didn't already know the answer.

She inclined her head to the figure on the ground beneath her. "He's hurt badly and—and he only meant to protect me. Please don't kill him."

Again, she offered only the simple request, as if Nama was someone she knew quite well...and trusted. Her voice shook with the aftereffects of her flight, not fear. Small wonder at that. They'd just been chased all over the Great School of Rome, up and down stairwells, through storage rooms, down corridors and across catwalks before they had been finally cornered. A flea and a wildcat.

"What about you?"

The woman's expression did not change.

"Your little Briton here must be completely out of his mind, or he would not have scaled the walls of the school to get *in*. The trainees here are all trying to find a way out."

"How do you know he's a Briton?"

"By his tattoos."

"Are you going to kill him?"

"Oh, no," he sneered. "Not just yet."

Her eyes widened. "What do you intend to do?"

Nama grinned.

Tears started to her eyes. "Please spare him."

The little mite had a one-track mind. "Why should I?" he spat.

"We meant no harm."

Nama barked a laugh so hard and so cold that both guards started. "I have six men dead. You call that no harm?"

"Your men kidnapped me and then chased both of us when Zerneboc tried to free me. He fought back out of instinct."

"Then he'll make an excellent gladiator," he said with a shrug. "I may take slaves from wherever I so desire. Your friend committed a crime when he scaled that wall, and the sentence calls for his death. Would you have me break the law?"

"I would have you show mercy," she replied without a shred of defiance. "Unless…"

"Unless what?" he challenged.

She bowed her head. "Unless that is not in your power to

extend."

"And if it isn't?"

"Then we have no choice but to die." She lifted her head and, after a momentary glance at the sword that hung at his side, looked him in the eye. "Be quick, but please, don't make him kill anyone."

Nama's eyebrows shot up for a second time, and he shook his head in disbelief. Was it courage or stupidity that made her so quiet, so accepting of her fate? They stood regarding one another for several long moments.

"What does she want, my lord?" one guard inquired.

"You heard her. She pleads for his life," he replied.

The guard snorted in derision and yanked his sword from its scabbard. "Let me at them, my lord!"

"No."

"But…" The guard pointed his weapon in consternation at the throatless body of a fellow soldier lying nearby.

Nama leveled a dark, withering stare on the unfortunate subordinate. The shorter man shrank down into his breastplate and withdrew his sword without further comment. Nama turned back to the woman.

"You are both spared," he said at last in Greek.

She heaved a sigh. "Thank you."

Nama stared at her and then scowled. "His arm will take time to heal. In the meantime, I suggest you pray to whatever gods you worship that it has been rendered useless, or by the Fates, he will be in the arena as a berserker with you tied to a stake as fodder. As I said, no one invades without punishment. You are both now my slaves. One small infraction of my commands can and will send you to the arena. You will do nothing, say nothing, *think* nothing unless I tell you to, is that clear?"

She bowed her head and nodded.

"Where are you from?"

The woman named a small Roman port on the northwestern Greek coast.

"You now belong to the Imperial School. What is your name?"

"May I tend to him?" she asked.

"I asked you a question, woman," Nama demanded. "I could give you a name, but I doubt you'd appreciate it."

"I am called Maus, my lord," she replied at last. "Please. May I tend to him? He bleeds."

"As do my men," he snarled.

Without taking his eyes from her face, Nama snapped his fingers at the guard on his right. "Gallus, send someone to clean up this mess and then take her and her companion to the infirmary. Let her deal with him. I don't need any more dead bodies on my hands. See that she has all she requires." To the woman, he said, "Go. Take what you need and keep him under control."

Without a second glance, he swept away.

TWO

Maus strained to get her companion up onto the stone slab that served for a table in the infirmary. He sagged against her like a heavy, limp, wet rag, his head lolling to one side. His slim build belied his genuine weight, and she struggled to stay upright. Together, they slipped in a puddle on the floor, and she lost her grip on him. He slumped over backward onto the slab with a heaving grunt.

Wiping her forehead, she pulled his feet up onto the slab and glanced around the room. A guard stood in the doorway, his arms crossed over his chest and his face set in a menacing glare. *No help from him, I'm guessing.* The dark man outside said to take what she needed, but for the life of her she didn't know if she knew what that was. She wasn't a physician. The biggest injuries she'd ever had to deal with were burns and the occasional slip of a fishing knife, but this…? With tattoos covering most of his body and dirt on top of them, it was difficult to discern exactly where all the blood was coming from.

"Water?" She wondered aloud.

Her eyes fell on a tall barrel standing in a corner of the room and something that looked like white cloth on a nearby shelf. *As good a place to start as any.* She took a step away from the slab, and a hand grabbed her wrist. She started.

Two unblinking obsidian eyes pivoted in her direction to search her face. A dark, long-haired head shook back and forth in a frantic negative.

She laid her hand over Zerneboc's and smiled reassuringly. "I'm not leaving."

His hand tightened and his eyes darkened even further in fear.

"I won't leave you," she repeated, this time laying her hand over his heart. "Don't be afraid."

Gradually, Zerneboc relaxed his grip. His eyes closed wearily. Maus went around the room as quickly as she could. Bandages, ointments, salves, splints, needles, and thread as well as some ominous looking knives lined the shelves and tabletops in the room. She dipped some of the water from the barrel into a basin, grabbed a stack of cloths from a shelf, and took them over to the slab where her companion lay. She returned to the shelves and pored over the various pots of ointment and salve, finally selecting one she prayed would fight infection.

The man opened his eyes when she approached and did not close them again the entire time she washed his wounds and cut away the tatters that were once the legs of his trousers. She marveled that he had so little injury after the heat of their flight and then grimaced at the sight of the festering skin and flesh of his upper left arm. It stank. Sand caked together with the oozing mess to form a nasty looking sludge. His fight with the guards had split open the long, deep wound that had only barely begun to close. She soaked the cloth in the water and laid it dripping on the wound in the hopes of loosening the filth while she inspected the rest of him. As she did so, her mind went back to the day she'd first seen him.

The thought of the horrible prison made her shudder even now, and the memory of bars and stone and unutterable suffering would never leave her. An iron bound wooden cube stood in the middle of the courtyard one stifling summer day some weeks after her arrival at the prison. Instinctual curiosity made her pause as she passed by it. The sound of guards made her hide away in a corner. The box looked barely big enough for a man to stand up in and the corners and sides looked as though it had been tumbled around loose on a ship.

A sadistic guard pounded on the side of the box and shouted obscenities into an open knot hole. The horrific shrieking that erupted from its interior made the hair on the back of Maus's neck stand on end. She clapped her hands over her ears. Whatever was inside that box thrashed wildly, rocking it back and forth. The guards laughed until a fist burst through the side of the cube and caught hold of the guard standing nearest. With a squelching wrench the man's neck snapped and his body went limp. The remaining guards fell silent and backed away as the creature inside the cube hammered it apart with his bare hands.

A nauseating stench roiled out of the wreckage. A short, powerfully built man rose to his feet. He was tattooed from the crown of his head to his ankles. Demonic figures and strange twisted symbols covered him in black and blue and orange and green ink giving him a terrifying appearance. His hair hung past his shoulders in matted braids. He slung them over his shoulder and faced his captors with a feral scream. Only then could Maus see the reason for the stench. Hanging from his upper left bicep was the putrefying remains of a rapidly decaying person. The two apparently had been born sharing an arm. His "twin" must have died in transit, leaving this poor wretch trapped and alone with death literally at his side.

To Maus's horror, what was left of Zerneboc's "twin" peeled off him when he stood up from the remains of the cube. Never had she seen such a thing! He slipped in the ooze when he tried to step forward and landed heavily on the ground on his left side. The sickening sound of snapping bone brought up her gorge. She turned away and vomited violently. When she could think again, she fled.

Later, she heard the guards tried four times to get near him to take away the body. Zerneboc lashed out in animal-like rage each time, maiming seven and killing five others. At last, they retrieved their wounded, backed the savage into a sandy area of the prison and erected heavy gates to keep him there as an object of torment. More than one prisoner was thrown to their death into what became known as "The Pit." The guards had been the ones to give him the name of Zerneboc, a name of Britannia. The Black Devil. Maus saw Zerneboc once the first day through a crack in the door as she hurried by with a bucket of slops. He was huddled under a bit of an overhang in "The Pit," and cradled his brother's corpse while rocking back and forth, whimpering like a whipped dog.

She shuddered as the memory washed over her and reality reasserted itself. Dark eyes looked up from the table into hers. "No wonder you're a little odd," she murmured to him.

Maus brushed the coarse black hair away from his face to dab water on the gash above his eye and the slice across his cheek. Zerneboc followed her movements with his eyes in complete silence. In all the time since she first met him, she had not heard him utter one word. He would grunt in question or reply, and he could hiss or shriek in anger or fear. But he never spoke. She wondered if he was even capable of it.

"You can hear, can't you?" she asked him softly.

He blinked and looked into her eyes in question.

"Yes," she chuckled. "I thought so."

His arm involuntarily twitched as she drew away the cloth on his arm. What a mess! She swallowed hard at the sight, dropped the soiled fabric to the ground, and then dipped a fresh cloth in the water and dabbed at his arm gently. It was a miracle he hadn't died of infection or gone mad. At least, he didn't have that hideous bone sticking out of him anymore. The wound took quite a while to clean out, but she finally managed to clear away most of the dirt and pus. Then she smeared it with the ointment.

"Are you two related?" The deep voice echoed off the stone enclosure.

Maus whirled around, nearly dropping a roll of bandaging as she did so. The African's massive frame loomed in the doorway. Zerneboc lunged up from the table, hissing in warning. Nama glared at him, but Maus laid a gentle hand on his shoulder. He moved no further but would not take his eyes off the man in the doorway.

"Are you related?" Nama repeated after a tense silence.

"No, my lord," she replied and began wrapping Zerneboc's arm.

"His wife? Concubine?"

"No."

"What then? Lovers?"

Maus shook her head with an embarrassed frown.

"You must mean something to him."

"He needed help." Silence again reigned for a long moment. "He still does," she added.

"Where did you find him?"

"He found me. I fell…into the pit…where he was kept."

"And you live?" The disbelief in his voice showed. "He broke the necks of two of my men and tore the throat out of another with his bare hands. Three more are dead of head and chest injuries. How is it that one little woman falls into the pit where he was kept and lives to talk about it?"

Maus hesitated before answering. The story of the Jewish prophet Daniel being thrown into a den of lions for praying to his God flashed into her mind. She knew that same God and His protection were the only reasons she hadn't been torn to pieces, and she should tell Nama so. The words, however, caught in her throat. Rome fed her enemies to the lions, too. None she knew of had ever survived.

"He trusts me," she managed instead.

"Oh, really? How is that?"

She turned to Zerneboc.

He regarded her with intense eyes.

"I don't know. Maybe because I speak *to* him, not *at*

him. He's aware of what I say and knows what I mean somehow. Maybe…it's something else." *Oh, God, forgive me. I am so afraid. I cannot tell him the truth. Help me! Give me courage!*

She could feel Nama watch her in silence as she continued to carefully pad and wrap Zerneboc's arm.

"Why do you tend him?" he demanded with a wave of his hand. "He's mad. Stricken by the gods. He cannot even speak!"

"He is not mad!" she rejoined hotly. "He's just…different." She turned to look the African in the eyes.

Nama arched a dark eyebrow.

"I can see why he was so anxious to get to you." He smirked.

She didn't respond.

"He saved your life." It was a statement, not a question.

Maus nodded.

"We were being held prisoner. Zerneboc digs like a mole. I crawled out through the hole he dug, and he followed. Been on the run since then until your men took me. You saw what he did today."

Nama gave a harsh bark of laughter. "Remind me to not put you two in a cell with a dirt floor." He changed the subject abruptly. "Are you finished?"

"Yes."

"Then follow me."

"Where are we—?"

"I said follow," he repeated in a tone that brooked no debate and turned away.

THREE

Nama tossed down the pen on his writing tablet and waved his hand to the guard at the door to his quarters to indicate his desire for privacy. As soon as the door shut, he stood and went to the window, letting his eyes run over the training grounds, barracks, walls, and the ever-vigilant guards that surrounded him. The sky twinkled with stars overhead. He hadn't realized how late it was. For a brief moment, he let his mind review the events of the day. Daily tallies. Letters. Training. Arrivals and departures. Deaths and burials. And last, but certainly not least, the Briton and his woman. He heaved a sigh and turned from the window. The woman.

Swahili. How long had it been since he'd heard the dulcet tones of his homeland? To hear them out of the little pale skinned female earlier that evening was…incredible. His heart and throat squeezed tight with unshed grief and regret. He'd not seen anyone of his tribe since his capture and sale to the editor of the Roman games twenty-three years ago. Almost ten years of fighting as a gladiator had earned him the position of head lanista, or trainer, for the Great School in Rome. Now, he trained others how to fight and how to die.

He ran a mammoth hand over his close-cropped hair and down over his face wearily and then shook his head.

He pondered the little female. Many women had come and gone in his time in Rome. Some even came to the Great School to train. There were those who willingly sold themselves for a night with a gladiator. Of the women forced to live at the School, few survived more than six months. Between the grueling labor and the brutal, broken, trapped masculinity surrounding them, women didn't last long. There was but one use for a woman to a man enslaved at Rome's gladiatorial school. This was no place for someone like this new frail little thing. Nama shook his head once more. His men were already placing bets whose bed she would warm first.

"Where did she learn Swahili?" he mused aloud. His was a nomadic tribe. Few in the Roman empire knew his people, much less his language, and none bothered to learn it. Greek was the common tongue of the masses.

She'd not shown an ounce of fear around that maniacal Briton or himself, and Nama had glared at her with all the force of his pent-up wrath. Yet she looked him in the eye and said thank you, not once, but twice! Once when he had spared her Briton and again when he had them locked away in their cell for the night. Incredible! He moved back to his stool in front of the writing table. Who was she? By the gods, he would find out.

"Gallus!" he barked. The guard at his door stepped into the room.

"Sir?"

"Bring me the woman."

Gallus' scarred face split into a cruel, knowing smile. He didn't have to ask which one. "What of the animal?"

"Just her."

"Yes, my lord."

"You sent for me?"

Nama turned and regarded the diminutive figure in front of him before waving Gallus from the room.

The door latch clicked shut behind Gallus.

Maus was bony with gray eyes and pale wispy red hair past her waist that looked as if it hadn't seen the right side of a comb in months. Small brown spots speckled her angular white face.

"How is it you know Swahili?" Years in a military environment had long robbed him of the gift of elegant speech.

"Sir?" Her confusion was very plain. As was her relief.

"Earlier. You spoke to me in Swahili, the language of my people. Where did you learn it?"

The woman's brow furrowed. "I—I don't understand,

my lord. I spoke in Greek."

"I *heard* Swahili."

"Y—yes, my lord, b—but I still don't understand. I am Thracian. I only know Greek. It is the language of my ancestors."

"What?" Nama barked when she paused.

Her throat convulsed audibly.

"What?" he barked, striding around the desk to tower over her. She seemed to shrink down into the floor.

"Unless it was God Who made you hear Swahili," she finished in an almost inaudible voice. Her hands shook, and she spoke with her eyes on the stones around her feet.

"God?" Here was the last answer he had expected. He gave a derisive snort of laughter. "There is no god."

The woman lifted her head and regarded him with gentle eyes. "All nature cries out that there must be a God, my lord."

Nama clenched his jaw. "I have been a lanista here for fourteen years. Do you know what that is?"

"No, my lord."

"A lanista," he spat. "Is a butcher. A butcher of men who trains others to be the same. I was a gladiator for a decade before that. I was beaten in battle. I disgraced my people. I've been whipped. Branded. Made to fight for the pleasure and entertainment of the filthy Roman mob. My people are murdered or scattered. Now I am a slave to their killers. I prayed to every god I knew when I first arrived. Where were any of the gods in all that time?"

"God's purposes are higher than mine, my lord." Her voice caught in her throat. "I don't know why He allows tragedy to happen."

Nama noted the sound of her voice. She had returned her eyes to the floor, but the anguish in her tone was unmistakable. He ground his teeth in impotent fury and remorse combined.

"Why would your god make me hear *your* words in *my* tongue?"

"Perhaps so you would spare my life," she replied quietly. "And the life of my friend."

"To what purpose?"

"I don't know."

Bitterness welled up within him. "So, your god likes torture then?" At her stricken look, he went on. "You will have little cause to bless me or this god of yours for keeping you alive. Slavery is not easy."

"I know."

"No, little mouse. You do *not*. You were better off on the run than here. Better still had you let me kill you as I intended. Gladiators are not like normal men. We have but one use for a woman, and it is not for religious chitchat. It is in my power to give you to any one of the men as a reward for a good performance in combat. I could even keep you for myself." He paused. Her face flamed red and then blanched white as marble at his bold, intimate perusal. He was the one shocked, however. She was embarrassed! Years had passed since he'd seen a woman embarrassed by anything. His eyes narrowed as he tried a different tack. "Or I could use your friend downstairs as a training tool. Of course, there wouldn't be enough left of him to bury after the first two rounds. Is that why your god spared you?"

Her head snapped up, eyes wide with dismay. Her chin trembled as a tear ran down each thin, freckled cheek. For the first time in years, Nama's heart smote him at the look of mute agony in her eyes. He turned away. Why should he care about the tears of a woman? Satisfied he had succeeded in terrifying her, he hardened his heart and his face. Let her be afraid.

"My God is able to save us and keep us from harm," a tremulous voice said from behind him.

Nama stiffened. He had heard words like that before. "And what god would that be?" he demanded quietly. The ensuing silence was deafening.

"The only God there is," came the reply.

The hair on the back of his neck stood up. Instinct had told him upon her arrival that this strange little woman would be different than the other slaves in the School. Now, her words were telling him she was a Christian. For some reason, that knowledge made his stomach lurch with fear.

FOUR

The chill morning air made Maus shudder beneath her thin woolen blanket. Always an early riser, she'd been staring up at the ceiling for quite a while from her mat in the small, locked cell she and Zerneboc shared. Normally, she would have enjoyed the rare moments of solitude she had, but today, the quiet felt oppressive. Not even prayer lifted the heaviness she felt. She sat up and tried to stretch.

"Ouch." With a grimace, she pulled a loose pebble out from under the heel of her hand.

Zerneboc roused at the sound of her voice, anxiously searching her face.

"I'm fine," she reassured him, pulling her blanket around her shoulders.

He lay back down. Even after weeks at the School, Zerneboc could not bear the weight of anything over him no matter the weather, and the only clothing he tolerated was a new set of ankle length trousers. His filthy feet were bare and hard as the stones he walked on. Maus leaned up against the cold wall of the narrow room and rubbed the pebble between her palms to warm her hands. She let her mind wander.

Zerneboc watched her every move. She gave him a wan

smile and then drew two stick figures in the dirt with the pebble.

"You," she told him and pointed to the first figure. He sat up on one elbow and regarded the picture solemnly from his corner. She pointed to the second stick figure and tapped her chest. "That's me."

When he did not move, she gave a small sigh and went back to her thoughts. She drew sea waves in the dirt with a tiny one-sailed vessel tossed to and fro atop them and then traced her stick figure inside it.

"See?" She explained and gave a faint-hearted laugh. "That's me and…" She drew a new figure with a long beard next to her. "A—and that's Alexandros. My brother." Tears burned her eyes.

Zerneboc's brow furrowed, and he cocked his head in question. Maus redrew his stick figure and added another attached to it at the arm.

"Brother," she started to say but Zerneboc growled low in his throat and smeared the picture with his hand. He huddled as far away from her as he could get, his callused feet scuffling against the hard packed floor. Maus reached out to comfort him, but he retreated even further, eyes glittering in the shadows with anger and pain.

She turned away and smoothed the dirt flat again. After a few moments, she redrew Alexandros and herself in the ship, arms joined. She cocked her head briefly and then traced a square around the picture. Next, she drew the ship tossed on angry waves with Alexandros outside the safety of the vessel. Then she drew a square around that picture as well. She kept on drawing, recreating in vignettes the days when life as she once knew it came to an end. Three days in a raging storm, alone on a ship out of control. A merchant vessel coming alongside what was left of the ship. Her sale to the keeper of the prison and her subsequent confinement. The keeper casting her into "The Pit" for refusing his advances and because her hair was red. She pulled at her hair. Many people thought red hair brought bad luck.

Scalding tears splashed into the dust until she could no longer see clearly. The sight of the memories she had so desperately tried to suppress shattered her outward calm. She dropped the pebble, covered her face, and burst into tears. She scrubbed the tears away angrily with the backs of her hands. *Why God? Why did You do this?* As if in answer, a tattooed hand came into view. She looked away, but Nama's face appeared in her mind's eye. *Alexandros would have been better at sharing Your love than I am. He was so good at speaking and inspiring others.* A choked sob escaped her at the remembrance of her elder brother sharing the Gospel of Jesus Christ with his fellow fishermen.

A quiet voice in her mind seemed to ask her, *Would you*

have had him die in an arena, little one?

Her tears flowed even harder at the thought of her much beloved sibling at the mercy of a gladiator or wild animal. Light began to glimmer in her heart. How great was God's compassion! Alexandros had been spared the fighting and she the agony of watching him hacked to pieces or burned alive or eaten. At least, she had the comfort of knowing he lived in Heaven with God with their mother and father. But, oh! How she longed to join him!

The tattooed hand moved slowly over to the very first picture she had drawn of Zerneboc and herself. A long finger redrew the figure of the man and then joined the lines between her arm and his. He paused, his still outstretched hand trembling slightly. Maus glanced up with another sob and met Zerneboc's uncertain gaze. With tears streaming down her face, she grabbed hold of his outstretched hand and pressed it to her heart.

"Brother," she whispered.

The days ran together until she lost all track of time. How long had she been in captivity? Three months? A year? Work started at dawn and did not end until the sun had gone completely from the sky. Maus and Zerneboc swept, raked sand, hauled wood and slops and laundry and dishes and water all day long until Maus thought she would drop. So far, the lanista had not followed through on his threat of turning her friend into a gladiator. Though his arm had healed, he remained at her side, silent and loyal. But for his presence and help, she would have collapsed with exhaustion.

The guards glowered anytime they went near them, their animosity palpable and their anger audible. Her fellow kitchen slaves and other staff held her at arms' length as well. She did her best to serve with quiet respect and dutiful attention, but her actions only seemed to make the dehumanized sufferers more detached and unfriendly. She prayed unceasingly for protection, for Zerneboc's salvation, for release, and for Nama who had been so generous with them both.

Each morning, she shared her life with Zerneboc in pictures and soon she found herself sharing about Jesus Christ, the Son of God. Maus told him how Jesus came to earth as a helpless child, grew and lived and suffered among humanity. She spoke of how He lived a sinless life and performed many miracles. How He died on a cross to take humanity's punishment for sin, was buried, and rose from the dead on the third day to become humanity's advocate with God the Father.

At first, Zerneboc shied away from hearing the name Jesus. He would sometimes even growl and hiss when she spoke it, but the longer Maus spent in captivity, the more her courage seemed to grow. Slowly and steadily, like a coal held close to flame, she persisted in prayer and speaking the truth of the one true God, telling her now adopted brother stories she had heard from Jewish Christians of God's prophets Isaiah and Daniel and Jeremiah, sent to warn His people of their impending doom if they did not repent and turn to Him. She told Zerneboc how God protected His people through men like Samson, King David, and Prince Moses. She told him what she knew of the Torah, God's holy Law.

Soon, he began to look for her to speak, until at last, he would place the pebble in her hand the moment she awoke in the mornings, gesturing eagerly for her to tell him more and sitting cross legged in front of her with childlike anticipation. He delighted to hear of battles won, of mighty men of valor, and of miracles, but he wanted nothing to do with the One from Whom all true miracles came. Weariness and despair at his rejection of Christ pressed in and down upon her heart.

"God loves me, Zerneboc," she whispered one cold rainy morning as they waited for the day to start. Her voice was hoarse with the damp chill in the room. There were times when that thought was all that kept her going day after grueling day. *God loves me, and Jesus gave His life for me.* The cell was dank and dark. She could hardly see to draw. Her hands shook and her teeth chattered. "H—he loves you and g—gave His life for you."

Zerneboc shook his head violently. She grabbed his hand and pulled on it to make him look at her.

"Yes! Yes, He did! Look." She pointed fiercely to the picture she had drawn of Jesus on the cross. "Look!"

Zerneboc threw the briefest of glances in the direction of the picture and stopped short. He turned back slowly. A strange sensation filled her, and she spoke with greater authority than she ever had before.

"God isn't willing that anyone should perish in Hell, but all men have sinned and come short of God's glory. Without Jesus, everyone is bound for that place of eternal torment and separation from God, but He loves everyone in the world so much that He sent His only Son to die in our place. Whoever believes on Him shall not die but have everlasting life. Can there ever be a greater love than someone laying down their life for another?"

Zerneboc's eyes widened to their fullest.

"He made me His child." She touched her heart. "He wants to make you His child, too. Repent and believe on Him, too. Please."

For a split second nothing in the little cell stirred. At first, Maus thought he hadn't heard her until even the sounds of the rain and the guards' ceaseless pacing faded away. Zerneboc sat motionless on his knees, staring at the picture of Jesus on the cross, one tattooed hand extended mid-air, head cocked as if hearing someone Maus could not see. Suddenly, his head snapped back. His whole body arched backwards as if in the grip of a mighty unseen hand and a horrifying shriek escaped him like the hissing of steam from under a pot lid. Maus threw an arm over her face and pressed herself back into the opposite corner in terror. Zerneboc convulsed once and then collapsed to the floor.

It took some moments before Maus could do anything but cower where she sat. At last, she lowered her arm and stared around the cell in utter shock, her mind a complete blank. Her breath came in ragged gasps. She shook her head to clear the ringing in her ears. What just happened? The sound of running feet and shouting snapped her out of her trance. She scrambled over to Zerneboc who lay on his side in the middle of the floor. Carefully, she turned him over, cradling his head in her lap. She stroked his face, her heart in her throat. He didn't move. She laid a trembling hand on his chest. Relief flooded her when she felt his heart still beating under her palm. At last, his eyes fluttered open, and a slow radiant smile spread across his tattooed face. Heavy keys rattled in the lock of the door and voices shouted.

"I…know…Jesus," he rasped, and the door crashed open.

FIVE

Nama stared across his writing table at the little woman in consternation. He didn't want to look at the Briton beside her. Just thinking about him made the hair on the back of the African warrior's neck prickle. The early morning watch had heard a commotion in their cell and rushed to investigate. Finding the Briton collapsed on the floor filled them with obvious elation, but they feared what their commander would do to them if anything happened, so they shook Zerneboc awake and dragged the two before him.

"You will not speak of this," Nama said in a dangerously quiet tone after dismissing the guards and hearing what Maus and her friend had to say. "Either of you. You will not speak of this God of yours. You will tell no one of this…this…"

"Miracle?" Maus supplied.

"Unbelievable occurrence," he corrected with a glare in the woman's direction. "Not now. Not ever. Is that understood?"

The woman remained silent, her head bowed, hands clasped in front of her, but the Briton spoke with barely contained joy. His voice came out in an even, perfect baritone as though he had always been able to speak.

"I cannot but speak of what God has done for me," he began.

"Silence!" Nama exploded out of his seat, his mammoth frame trembling with the effort it took to regain self-control. He took a shaking breath. What manner of God was this that could give a mute his voice? He regarded Zerneboc in awe. The man's eyes were the most disturbing of all. Instead of their normal obsidian vacancy, they were clear gray and glowing with…what?

"You are Christian." It was not a question.

Both slaves nodded.

"You know what happens to Christians when they are captured."

Again, they nodded, but Nama felt the need to list the horrors perpetrated against the followers of the religion known as The Way despite the two slaves' calm acceptance.

"They die the deaths of the lowest criminals. They are fed to lions or packs of wild dogs. Tortured. Crucified. Used as torches. This is the fate you would wish upon yourselves?"

Neither answered, and he turned away from their peaceful expressions in disgust. He found the quiet surrounding them disconcerting to say the least. He strode over to his window and stood gazing out with his hands clasped behind his back.

"You are both watched," he began after a few moments'

pause. “Especially you, little mouse. There are things and people I cannot protect you from. You may not say much, but what you *do* shouts volumes. You cannot possibly be ignorant of the jealousy that surrounds you. And you…” He gestured at Zerneboc and shuddered inwardly yet again. “Gallus has not forgotten what you did when you arrived. Those were friends of his you mutilated that night. He would gladly see you both fed to the lions or dogs or crucified if he could manage it. If you persist in sharing this socially aberrant religion of yours, you’ll just be giving him the hammer and nails to hang you with. I want your word that you will speak to no one of this God or what has occurred this morning.”

“We cannot give you that, my lord,” Maus replied. “I’m sorry.”

“I am not submitting a request to the Roman Consulate, woman!” Nama shouted. “I am commanding you not to speak of it.” Ink and wine splattered as he cleared his writing table of its contents with a sweep of his arm. “Did you not hear what I just told you? Do you both have a death wish?”

Zerneboc stepped forward. “We are given the command by Almighty God to share the good news of Jesus Christ, my lord. Our God is able to deliver us, but if He wills that we die, we know that we shall live with Him forever in Heaven with Christ. This is why I now choose a new name. Joshua.

'Our God Saves.'"

Nama stared. "Why?" He managed at last. "You are slaves. No freedom. No rights. No future. What decent God would allow faithful followers such as you to suffer and die? What God could possibly be so important to you that you would risk such a death?"

Maus smiled, but it was Joshua who spoke. "We follow the only God there is. Jesus Christ is the Son of the Living God. He suffered and died for us to save us from our sins. How can we do anything but give our lives to Him in return?"

Nama drew back, unable to respond for the fear welling up inside him. Something in the Briton's shining countenance and humble statement made him shudder like no other opponent in the arena had ever been able to do. He had seen countless Christians die, and it had never affected him. In fact, he held them in derision. Only cowards stood and let an animal or gladiator take them down without a fight. Why then did these two disturb him now? Why should their fate so concern him that he was beginning to lose sleep over it? He'd worked with berserkers like the Briton before and sent them to die in the arena without the least compunction. How many women had he abused in all his years in Rome?

If the truth be told, he knew in the core of his being that he feared their God more and more with each passing day.

First, he heard Swahili from a woman who did not speak it. Now he saw a man born mad and mute, now, sane and able to speak as a direct result of this God's power. A silence so deep it could be felt fell over the room. It was as if someone else had entered unannounced. Someone with great authority and terrible power. That someone stood waiting. Waiting for him.

The silence grew agonizing.

"You may go," he croaked.

Nama paced his quarters like a caged animal after the two left. Of all the stubborn, thick headed… What were they thinking? He threw himself onto the stool in front of his writing table and absently picked up the wine goblet from the floor with a short laugh. Why did he care? He'd asked himself that a thousand times. Why did he continually call for her when he knew she would speak of her God? What was her God to him? Joshua's face loomed up in his mind's eye, and he shoved himself to his feet once more. The Briton's God now, too.

Nama had not touched her since her arrival, though plenty of opportunities had presented themselves. He wouldn't suffer anyone else to touch her either, making it seem as though she were his woman. This seemed to fan the fires of jealousy that swirled around her. He did not care. She *was* his woman even if he wouldn't touch her. His instincts had served him well in the arena, and they told him that to do her harm would bring the wrath of her God upon him. Unfortunately, others more influential than himself did not share his intuition. Even a slave like Gallus could hold the ear of a capricious lord, and the guard would use that ability out of vengeance or spite.

"My God is able to save us and keep us from harm," the woman had said on her first night at the School. He found himself wishing that were true. Her quietude and dependability were unheard of gifts in a place such as the Great School where every kind of evil was practiced and none could be trusted. Her presence served to soothe the ever-present depthless ache that daily threatened to consume him. He watched her serve him and others no matter what their reaction might be, and he had seen Gallus' resentment build. He summoned her repeatedly to help him in his chambers or his library and somehow always the conversation seemed to turn to this God and to Jesus. He ran a dark hand over his head and sighed.

Jesus. If ever there was a name that could turn an entire world upside down, that name was it. Even the Emperor knew of Jesus…and hated him. Some called this Jesus a magician, some other things far less polite. Nama had heard it said once that the man was a lowly Jewish carpenter. Most said he was just a man who simply got in the way of jealous religious leaders. To the woman, however, he was the son of her God come in the flesh, restored to life after allowing himself to be crucified and now ascended into the heavens. He rubbed his chest. His heart burned strangely whenever he thought about that.

He went again to his window and gazed out. The mid-morning sky was cloudless and full of glorious sunshine. An acute sense of longing filled him as he stared out at the crystal blue expanse. For what did he long? Suddenly he felt inexplicably weary, but he pushed away from the feeling out of habit, calling to a slave to come clean up the mess on the floor. He almost called again for Maus but shook his head. He'd had enough of that for one day. A good soak in the baths and some wine would clear his head…He ran a hand over his face and shook himself. At this time of day? What was he thinking? There was too much to do. *I've been in this accursed hole far too long. I'm going mad.*

SIX

"Three nights ago, I had a dream," Joshua said as he and Maus swept out a cell and readied it for an arriving prisoner. She glanced up at him in surprise.

"Why did you not tell me before?" she asked, dumping the rubbish into a pail.

Joshua's smile was gentle and sweet. "I've been praying over it. In my dream, I saw my village and the house where I was born. My father stood in front of the door to the roundhouse calling my name and saying, 'We are empty. We are empty. Come home! Come home!'"

Maus shook her head. "I have no head for such things," she said with a sigh. "What do you suppose that means?"

"That is why I spent three days in prayer," Joshua replied as he gave the sand on the floor to the cell a final raking. "I believe God is calling me back to my people, little sister. My tribe knew my brother and me. They knew our ferocity in battle. They heard us take the blood oaths and sacrifice to false gods. They saw the demons take us and use us to do horrible things in the name of Satan. And not only us, but others also. I remember the black despair I felt before Christ redeemed me, and my heart is burdened for my people."

Maus busied herself with filling the fresh water bucket at the well in the center of the courtyard. A piercing sadness filled her, and she could not reply. Part of her rejoiced to watch this adopted brother of hers grow in strength and humility even if it did mean more ostracizing by the people around them who now counted them cursed as well as shown favoritism. Joshua's nearness and companionship were joys made double now that he was also a brother in Christ. But part of her was also afraid. Memories of losing another brother filled her mind, and she fought the despair threatening to overcome her.

"You're sure God's called you away?" she asked in a voice that she prayed did not shake.

"Yes," he replied simply and pulled the bucket over the side of the well. "I have prayed and cannot escape the thought that my people need to hear the Good News of Jesus Christ, and I am the one to tell them."

Fear welled up inside her. "But…won't they…" She couldn't finish.

Joshua looked down at her with clear, gray eyes. "My people are enslaved to Satan, little sister. How can I not share the Good News of salvation with them, even if it means I die?"

A cook barked at them to get moving and not waste

time. For the rest of the day, Maus fought her inner turmoil as she struggled to keep up with her work. At length, her own strength spent, she sought God. *Forgive me, Father. You have protected us this far. Even if we are to die, You will give us the strength we need when we need it. Help me not to be afraid or to forget why I'm here. I surrender myself and Joshua to You and entrust ourselves to Your ever tender care.* The struggle inside her began to ebb, and peace took its place. Maus drew a long breath and smiled. A guard gave her a confused, almost frightened, look.

That night after their meager meal, Joshua leaned back against their cell wall and breathed deeply. "We will not be in slavery much longer, little sister." He shifted from one hip to the other. "I can hardly keep still thinking of it. As soon as we're released, we will first seek out fellow Christians here in the city. Once we have learned more of Jesus, we will return to my people."

Maus tugged her blanket around her and bit her lip to keep from crying. "D—do you know when you'll be released?"

"Not just me, little sister. *We.* We will be released together."

Maus blinked. "What?"

Joshua grinned at her. "God sent me a second dream last night. My father was again at the front of our home calling for me as in the first dream. But this time, I went to him, and he grasped my arm in welcome. Then he held out his hand in welcome to you and kissed your cheek like a daughter." He turned to look down at Maus. "You see, my mother was said to have had hair just like yours. It will be like an omen to my people. A good omen."

Maus tingled in sheer delight. She could hardly dare to hope what Joshua said could be true until a verse from the Hebrew Scriptures came to her mind. "In the mouth of two or three witnesses, let every matter be confirmed," she murmured.

Joshua cocked his head in question, so she repeated the quote. His face split into a wide smile. "Indeed!"

"When will it happen, do you think?" she queried. "How?"

"I don't know," he said, taking her hand and holding it to his heart. "But whatever happens, it is sure to be an act of God."

Maus sobered instantly. "Yes," she agreed. Few slaves ever left the School alive.

SEVEN

If ever the stars had converged to curse him, it was now. Nama swore under his breath. The morning started with the arrival of the editor of the Games at Ephesus. The day did not improve after his entrance to the Great School of Rome. A heavy set and pernicious man, the editor ate and talked incessantly, and his entourage filled the corridors making the daily routine nearly impossible. The guest seemed wholly unaware of the chaos he created.

"The crowd in Ephesus grows impatient with the traditional nets and swords," he was telling Nama after they had dispensed with formalities. "I need something more eye-catching."

"Such as?" Nama inquired, pretending to not know what the editor meant.

"Something savage," the editor replied, wiping his fat, greasy fingers on his nearest servant's robe. "Mind you, I have all the beasts I can handle. I'm looking for some*one*."

Nama inclined his head. Immediately the Briton came to mind. His heart sank, but he did not let his thoughts show in his expression. The editor snapped his fingers, and a slave poured him a large goblet of wine.

"I need other things as well. We're low on Gauls just now and Germans. When can I see what you've got?"

"Immediately if you wish." Nama waved him toward the door.

"Excellent!"

Nama led him through the corridors of the School and out onto a balcony overlooking a practice ground where two gladiators with staves were locked in combat. The two lanistas stood observing the gladiators in silence for several moments. The mid-day sun beat down hot on them, and the obese Ephesian was already sweating from the exertion of walking despite the shade a slave offered with a palm frond. Nama smiled inwardly. *Let him sweat. The more uncomfortable he is, the sooner he'll leave.*

"I heard you acquired a young Briton some months back," the editor panted as the gladiators attacked each other again. "Six kills to his credit. Singlehanded."

Nama arched an eyebrow in the older man's direction, silently cursing his continuing ill luck. Trust Gallus to run his mouth. Fool that he was, he should never have sent the vindictive guard to receive the Ephesian from the Emperor's palace. Keeping his face carefully neutral, he shrugged with feigned indifference. "Nothing spectacular. He turned out to be good for nothing more than hauling refuse."

"Six kills and you have him dragging garbage?!"

"His arm was infected when he came into my possession. He healed well enough, but the infection rendered his arm useless for combat. Affected his mind, too. Made him too…passive."

"Hmph! Passive can be corrected. And it's only one arm after all. He can probably still fight if he was that savage to begin with. What made him kill in the first place?"

"We never truly narrowed that down," he lied easily. "But whatever the reason, I couldn't very well present a timid, gibbering fool with a dead arm to the mob, could I? Hardly good for business."

"I see." The editor twirled one of the expensive rings encircling his left index finger. "What made you keep him?"

Nama grinned. "Someone has to take out the trash."

The Ephesian sipped his wine and returned no reply. Nama besought every god he could think of to turn the editor's mind away from the Briton. The last thing this vile man needed to know was Joshua's Christianity. To Nama's relief, the discussion turned to the two gladiators in front of them and the possibility of a Gaul savage enough to keep the mob in Ephesus sated for a few games.

"A pity that Briton of yours couldn't have been salvaged," the editor remarked as he prepared to leave for the day. "I heard he tore the throat out of one man. He would have been perfect."

Nama nodded his assent stiffly and motioned for the Ephesian to take the lead through the door. The cruel smile and eager blood lust in the man's eyes sickened him. Despite his occupation and years of dealing in slaves and blood sport, Nama had no taste for the extent of this man's brutality.

EIGHT

Maus stared wide-eyed at Nama. "N—nothing," she stammered. "I touched nothing, my lord. Certainly nothing so valuable as a ring. I know the punishment for theft. Besides, God…"

The lanista cut her off. "Spare me. It's enough I have to suffer this repugnant Ephesian's presence without throwing your religion on top of it all. Tell me plainly, why did you take the ring?"

"I did not, my lord. I have not seen it, much less touch it."

"Then how do you explain this being found in your cell?" Nama held up a heavy silver ring. "The gem is missing. A ruby."

Maus stared dumbfounded. A cold dread filled her. "I don't know, my lord," she whispered.

Nama sighed in exasperation. "Gallus says otherwise. He says he has three witnesses that all say they saw you hiding something in your hands when you left these chambers yesterday. The editor's ring disappeared around the same time. He had your cell searched and found the ring."

Maus could offer no words in her own defense. It didn't

matter that it would be sheer insanity for a slave to attempt to steal anything here and stupidity to then hide it where it could be so easily found. Add to that, she wasn't allowed anywhere near the front gates of the School or that she and Joshua both hadn't been outside it in months where they would have had the opportunity to pawn the jewel. They were being set up, and it was obvious. Worse, there was nothing they could do. She felt nauseous.

"Where did the gem go?"

When she shrugged wordlessly, Nama gestured to one of his guards, his face like black granite. "Search her."

Tears of humiliation slid down her cheeks as she stood naked before the guard who rifled her threadbare tunic and headscarf. Her hands trembled when he thrust the worn garments back at her without a second glance. She covered herself as quickly as she could.

"Nothing there, sir," the guard informed Nama.

The lanista waved him from the room. He looked down upon her and chewed his lip in silence for a long time. At length, he sat on the edge of his writing table with his arms folded over his chest and gave a short mirthless laugh.

"What did you have in your hands yesterday?"

Maus couldn't reply for her tears.

"*Did* you have something in your hands?"

She nodded.

"Well? Don't make this harder than it already is. What was it?"

"A bird," she sniffled.

"A what?"

"A bird, my lord. It must have hit the window and stunned itself. I took it downstairs and released it."

Nama sighed heavily, rubbing his forehead and face wearily. He said nothing for a long time.

"Why is this Jesus of yours so hard to hide?" he muttered at last. "A simple Jewish carpenter. Why couldn't he be like any other self-respecting god and stay safely on Mount Olympus with the rest of the other socially acceptable deities?"

Maus' heart went out to him. His internal struggle was evident in his face. *Please, dear Jesus. Please help him. Help me!*

"I cannot seem to keep your Christianity under wraps, little mouse," he went on. "And the gods know I've tried." His normally hardened features softened as he gazed down into her face. "I don't want to have to be the one to kill you. You're the only one I trust in the accursed place!" He pounded the table with his fist and started to pace. "That thrice blasted Ephesian has asked countless questions about you and your Briton. He's worse than a dog with a bone! I've no desire to see you dead, but the gods won't hear me!"

At her master's words and the look in his eyes, her heart warmed. He had seemed preoccupied to her even before the Ephesian guests had come. Now she knew the Holy Spirit had been at work in his heart. She sought to reassure him.

"I am in God's hands, my lord. So is Joshua. He alone is able to rescue us from this man, and no power on earth can separate us from Him or His love. God will prevail, my lord. That I know. I did not take the ring. Neither did Joshua. We have no proof but our previous honesty and trustworthy conduct."

Nama held her eyes for a long time. The longing in them made Maus want to weep.

"If I thought, for a moment, that the Editor wouldn't hunt you both down the minute you left this place, I would free you both."

NINE

The door crashed open so hard it rebounded on the entering crowd.

"Did you find it?" The words were being spoken even as the Ephesian editor swept into the room, his entourage and personal guard behind him.

Nama sat down behind his writing table and leveled a stony glare at the fat man before him and said nothing.

"Well?" The editor demanded.

Nama glared at the man in utter contempt. "The woman has been searched. She does not have it. Satisfied?"

"No! Your guard saw the woman take it. If she does not have it, then the Briton must!" The editor turned to his guard. "Search him! Now!"

While he regarded the Ephesian with outward calm, the sound of tearing fabric and the cries of the woman made Nama's blood boil. The gods had failed him yet again. For the first time since his capture, he felt the control on his panic beginning to slip and in the depths of his heart, he besought the woman's God for the first time. *Jesus. Holy One. If You will deliver Your servants from this man, I swear to You, I will set them free.* An inexplicable calm settled over him. He locked eyes with his nemesis from Ephesus.

Nama straightened. What had he just seen Gallus do? It had been a slight movement, but Gallus pulled something from his belt and started to tuck it into Joshua's trousers as he pretended to search them.

"Just a moment." Nama stood to his full height and came around the table. He caught Gallus' left wrist. "What is this?" he asked with deadly calm.

The smaller man startled. "My lord?"

Nama tightened his grip and twisted upward making it impossible for the guard to release what he had in his hand. "A little something in your hand is there, Gallus?"

"Y—yes, my lord," Gallus stammered. "I found it in the Briton's pocket."

Nama nodded in feigned sympathy. "I'm sure. Especially since there are no pockets in these trousers." His grip on the smaller man's wrist tightened further. Bones ground together. A nerve in Nama's cheek twitched. "Give it to me."

"M—my wrist…"

Nama let go of Gallus' wrist as if it were poisonous. He yanked a small leather pouch from his hand in the same motion and strode back to his desk. "You were the one who claimed to have seen the woman take something from this room, were you not, Gallus?"

"Yes, my lord," he replied, massaging his wrist.

"Did you stop her or at least follow her? Make certain that she had it?"

"No, my lord. I had to remain at my post."

"Did you immediately send someone to search her cell? Her garments? Her person? And what of the Briton?"

"Well, no, but…"

"What is the point of all this meaningless questioning over two worthless slaves?" The Ephesian interrupted. "Is it not enough that the ring was found on the Briton? Give him to me, and we'll forget this whole unfortunate event ever happened."

Nama ignored him. "By your own admission, Gallus, you were outside this room when the theft occurred. Yet you sent no one to make sure of what you saw, and I just caught you putting evidence on the accused person's clothes."

He snapped his fingers, and two of his own guards from the corridor stepped into the room. "Search him," he commanded, never once taking his eyes from Gallus as the men took their fellow soldier by the arms and reached for his armor. Gallus' eyes flickered as they stripped off his clothing piece by piece. He held his silence until one reached for a leather cord hanging around his neck.

"No!" he cried out, fighting his captors.

Nama hooked a finger around the cord and pulled it out

from the smaller man's tunic. A cloth bag hung at the end. With a flick of his wrist, he jerked the bag from around the guard's neck and emptied the contents into his hand.

"Nice," he said sardonically, fingering the golden coins. "Enough to buy your freedom."

"It was the editor's idea," Gallus gabbled out. "Not mine. He paid me to do it!"

"Shut your mouth, you stupid fool!" the Ephesian spat.

Nama turned on the editor.

"How dare you come in here making threats and accusations?" Nama spoke with deadly calm. "Thinking to steal from me?"

The Ephesian blinked in surprise. "Your slave steals from *me*," he blustered. "And you have the nerve to make such a statement? You arrogant…"

"Don't." Nama waggled his finger back and forth in front of the smaller man's face. He carefully put the coins back in the cloth bag and stuffed them into the editor's fat fist along with the jewel from his ring. "Just don't. I've had all I can stomach from you. You have your Gaul and your German. Now get out."

TEN

Joshua put his arm around Maus' shoulders and drew her close to his side as the guards hauled Gallus screaming from the room. She had begun to tremble violently, so he held her close lest she fall. Her eyes bespoke the terror she must be feeling. He knew well the guard's fate was unenviable. He also knew she was praying for him. Recalling the visions God had sent, Joshua prayed too, for wisdom and a clear path.

Nama slammed the heavy door behind the retreating Ephesian editor, muttering under his breath, "The last we'll see of him and good riddance!" After two steps into the room, he turned on his heel, jerked the door open again, and shouted at a passing servant, "You there! Bring food and wine for three!" He slammed the door shut again and strode over to his writing table.

Maus' head collapsed onto Joshua's shoulder and her eyes closed wearily. A moving of the Holy Spirit stirred within him. *Today, Lord God? After so many months of praying and waiting, is it today?* A small smile pulled at the corners of his mouth at the thought.

"What are you grinning at, Briton?" Nama demanded as

he strode back to the door yet again and handed a scrap of paper out it to a slave and barked the order, “Make it quick!”

Joshua’s smile only broadened. Something inexplicable welled up in his heart and filled him with an excitement he had never felt before.

Nama cocked an eyebrow and pursed his lips. He waved a massive hand in the direction of a couch near a heated brazier. “Sit,” he commanded and stalked past them into his bedchamber, returning moments later with a sleeping rug.

“Wrap her in that,” he said and thrust it at Joshua.

Joshua pulled the voluminous fur covering around Maus’ shoulders, tugging some of it over her head. Her white face peeped out of its folds like a worn ivory carving. The telltale lines of exhaustion showed around her eyes and mouth. Today had been draining for them both. He eased her down on the couch and put his arms around her to help warm her.

Nama sat down at his desk and pulled out quill, ink, and paper. He thought for some moments before committing words to print. No sooner had he put his quill to the parchment when a knock sounded at the door.

“What?” he bellowed.

Two servants entered, one with a tray laden with food and the other bearing two hefty bundles in his arms.

“Lay them down and get out,” the lanista said without looking up. The servants obeyed with haste and left. He scribbled something on the bottom of the first parchment, shoved it aside, and began on the second. After several minutes of silence, Nama said, "Don't just sit there. Eat. No. Dress first and then eat. I know how prudish you Christians can be." He looked pointedly at the shreds of Joshua's worn trousers he had attempted to tie around his waist after the guards searched him. "Footwear will come later."

Joshua released Maus and picked up the bundle closest to him. The folds of a new tunic sprang upwards as he loosened the knot tied in the thick wool cloak wrapped around it. The floor length garment was soft and clean. A beautiful belt and head covering lay neatly folded underneath it. His heart gave a great leap at the sight. God was already preparing their way.

"Yours, I think," he said, and held out the bundle to Maus.

The second bundle held trousers and a shorter tunic, a wide leather belt, a money scrip, and a cap tied together in a warm cloak similar to the first. Joshua looked up from his new clothes to see Maus cover her face with her cloak and burst into tears. He took her gently into his arms as her shoulders shook.

"Shh, little sister," he soothed, stroking her hair. "'Our God shall supply all our needs according to His glorious riches in Christ Jesus', remember? Already He is preparing the way for us. See?"

"I know," she said in a muffled voice. "I'm just so very…oh, I don't even know how to say it." She gave a feeble laugh and managed a crooked smile.

He smiled and with his thumb smoothed away the tears that continued to run down her cheeks. The look in her eyes made him suck in a sharp breath. *Oh, Lord God.*

"You will remain in my chambers tonight," Nama's voice cut through his thoughts. "As soon as that fool of an Ephesian is on his way, I will send you to a safe place I know in the outskirts of the city where you can hide until you both can board a ship for Britannia. And don't worry. The proprietor of the inn I'm referring to is also a Christian. He will be able to make the necessary preparations for supplies and safe passage." He paused and gave a soft chuckle. "Don't look at me like that, little mouse. I swear on my life that I'm telling you the truth."

Maus stared up at him, speechless, but Joshua's heart soared. He hugged her to him in his excitement. "Thank You, Jesus!" he cried. "'Praise Him for His wonderful works to the children of men!'"

Nama nodded in solemn assent. "Your God is greater than any I have ever encountered," he said. "I prayed to the gods of Rome, to the gods I served all my life as a gladiator, even to the gods of my people, and none of them heard me. I know now they cannot hear me. I prayed to your Jesus, and He delivered you this day when all seemed hopeless. I promised Him I would free you." Maus gasped as Nama laid down his pen and held out a sealed scroll to each of them. "And I have kept my word. Documents of manumission. You are no longer my slaves. You will both leave here free people."

Maus rose and approached the lanista. Weeping for joy, she fell at his feet, took his dark hand in her own, and kissed it. Then she held it to her cheek. Nama scowled, the muscles in his jaw working.

"Get up," he ordered hoarsely. He sniffed loudly as he looked them both up and down. "You will bathe…" He wrinkled his nose in disgust. "Tonight. The woman will use my chambers."

"Thank you," Joshua replied for them both and took the scrolls.

The next few hours seemed like a dream to Joshua. Washed and attired in new clothing for the first time in his entire life, he felt like a dream walker. Nama waved him to a seat on a couch and bade him eat. Roast pork, fresh apples, grapes, pears, bread, and wine lay on a tray before him. His head spun. Feeling stunned, he took some of the bread and half an apple and then sat staring at them in mild bewilderment. At last, he took a bite of the fruit. The sweetness that filled his mouth overwhelmed him. He sucked on each piece, savoring the tart taste to the utmost.

Nama sat up on the couch on which he had reclined.

Joshua turned as Maus stepped out of Nama's chambers and entered the room.

Her waist length, auburn hair was combed out and loosely braided. Curling wisps framed her lovely face. Her head covering lay draped over her shoulders like a shawl. Joshua felt his mouth drop open in wonderment. She looked like an angel. Nama laughed and clapped him on the shoulder.

"You'd better claim her now, Briton," the lanista remarked, raising his wine cup in salute. "Before *I* do."

Joshua rose and went to her, his heart in his throat. *Oh, Heavenly Father!* he prayed. Maus held out her hand to him, and he took it between both of his own. He could hardly think past the thundering of his own heart, but when he looked down into her face, he saw his own desire mirrored in her eyes. Joy filled him to overflowing. As a freeman, he could at last make his own decisions.

"I do," he whispered to her, touching his forehead to hers. "I *do* claim you as my wife."

Three days later, Joshua stepped out of the Great School

of Rome for the first time since he had scaled the wall to rescue his lady. Even under the cover of darkness, the City of the Seven Hills felt oppressive, and the crowded buildings nearly overwhelmed him until he felt a slender hand grasp his own. His wife looked up into his face with a sad smile. He looked back over his shoulder. In the moonlight, he saw a tall, dark figure atop the School's stone wall, arms crossed over his great chest. Joshua met Nama's gaze and nodded. The lanista jerked his chin in farewell. Maus wept in silence.

"With God, all things are possible," he reminded her. He put his arm around her shoulders, knowing how his wife's heart was breaking. Nama had not accepted Christ. "We will pray. Always. God knows."

With those words, he took a deep breath and turned to follow the guards that would take them to the outskirts of the city. God had supplied everything they needed and more than he had ever dreamed. Today would be the start of their journey home. Home to share the Good News with his family and his people. So many things still needed attending to, but he knew God would continue to provide. That knowledge filled him with joy unspeakable and peace that passed all his previous understanding.

The End

"The name of the LORD is a strong tower: the righteous runneth into it and is safe."

Proverbs 18:10

THE SAGA OF LITTLE WELL

God's Love Transforms

Once, a little spring of water came to live in a beautiful valley bordered by mountains. For years the waters under the earth pushed up and up until at last, a tiny bubbling spring burst forth into a little basin in the shadow of a rock. Her muddy waters from the journey upwards spilled past the rock until at last, a cool, clear pool appeared.

"I am Little Well," she burbled to the world.

The Valley around her swarmed with beautiful things. Throughout the summer, the warm scents of daffodils and sun-drenched grass wafted her way. Autumn breezes combed the trees, carrying away their brilliant red gold foliage and decorating her waters with festive hues. Amidst them, bandit-eyed Raccoon and naked-tailed Opossum came to her for a drink. While sleek Otter grew too big to share in her waters, Squirrel the Chatterbox and Stealthy Fox often paused on her banks on their way to winter dens. Winter snow and sleet made Little Well sleepy, and her face grew dark with ice.

Spring sunshine woke Little Well to the advent of warmth and growth each year. She stretched her waters out over their banks as the winter's snows loosened their hoary grip on her. She gurgled happily as bees and birds once more flitted overhead.

Little Well learned the name of every tree, insect, and

animal that passed by her. She learned their habitats and their migration routes. As for the beings themselves, she neither knew nor cared. Only knowing about them mattered to her. Soon, few knew as much as she.

"My waters are the best in all the Valley," she told herself. "I don't have to draw from Maw the River like every other well. I know when the herds and songbirds come long before anyone else." She chuckled.

Spring and winter passed. Rain and sunshine came and went. Sun and moon rose and set. All was as it had been from her beginning. Though for a time, her waters remained sweet, she did not grow any deeper. For a long time, she did not notice any difference. The horses showed the change first, wrinkling their silken noses at her waters.

"What is it?" she asked one of them.

But the graceful creature snorted and shied away. Soon, the deer avoided her and then the birds, until by degrees even the insects buzzed over her without stopping. The field mice, who were known to eat or drink anything, chattered and mocked, calling her Mara.

"Your waters are horrible!" one squeaked.

"Nasty bitters!" chittered another. "Nasty Mara." And they threw dirt and dead grass at her.

Little Well grew angry. "What have I done to deserve this? My waters have always been the best in the valley."

"So you like to tell us," the first mouse replied. "But not anymore."

"Yes," the second mouse added. "There are other wells in the Valley. We don't have to come to you."

Little Well was shocked. No one had ever questioned her self-sufficiency before. "Those field mice are such liars. Surely someone needs me."

But no one returned to her. Even the cleansing rain deserted her. The green, oozing scum of envy crept in and sullied her waters. The little birds courted and raised young in the nearby trees, but she had no one. The bees and other insects twittered back and forth to one another in the long green grass.

"Why is it that I sit here all alone? I would be a good friend to someone if they only gave me a chance. Look how much I know." She looked around, listening with a hopeful ear. But alas, no one was interested in what she knew.

With each season that passed her over, she saw everyone else had some reason for being. Bee and Ladybug whirred with joyful hum from flower to flower, tending the wild flowers swaying in the breeze. Mockingbird and Cardinal filled the air with the loveliest of serenades, cheering the hearts of weary travelers as well as protecting their nests. Cricket and Hare announced to the fields the approaching twilight.

But what did she do? Where was her joy? Her sweet waters were sweet no more. Now they were murky and shallow. In her little alcove of earth, few if any could see her.

At last, her heart hardened, and her waters turned sour. Weeds and unpleasant, eyeless worms began to encroach on her banks. The once friendly sun baked her soft brown borders to a cracked, stinking hole. She shuddered and drew deeper into the embankment on the side of the field, peeping out on the world and feeling very unhappy indeed. Why was this happening to her? She didn't deserve to be treated this way.

Lower down in the field and below where Little Well lived, reigned the mighty River Maw. All who passed through the field were forced to ford his foaming currents. His plentiful waters supported the yearly salmon runs, towering bulrushes, and thousands upon thousands of animals. Herds stopped to take their fill at his banks as they passed by on their long treks southward. Even in the darkest winter nights when the Aurora rippled overhead, his waters never paused in their rush to the Great Sea.

"How beautiful are my waters," he boasted with a roar. "Come one and all to me, and I will satisfy you."

Little Well sighed. Maw had a right to brag of his prowess. The magnificent black stallion, Morning Star, brought his herd down from the plateau to the river every day to drink. He would stand in Maw's foaming rapids and watch over his mares and foals as they partook of the quieter waters downstream, his white mane flowing back over his ebony sides. Everyone knew Morning Star did not bring his people just anywhere.

One day, as the other horses took their fill, their chief matriarch, Myrrh brought her newest foal past Little Well to graze.

"Good day," Myrrh said with a stately bow of her russet head.

Little Well rippled her waters in surprise. Many days had come and gone since anyone had spoken to her. She gave a glum twitch of her surface in reply.

The little dun filly's ears shot forward at the sound, and she timidly drew nearer Little Well.

"What a funny whinny you have!" said the filly.

"That's not a whinny. Those are bubbles. See?" She rippled her waters at the filly who in turn snorted playfully, pawing the ground and sidestepping the edge of her waters with dainty hooves.

"What is your name?" the filly asked.

Little Well gave her name with a disinterested sigh.

"I am the Princess Sunrise, daughter to Morning Star and Myrrh. Will you play with me?"

Little Well drew down her waters in sullen frustration. "Wells don't play."

"Why not?"

"Because I, well, we don't have anyone to play with."

"I'll play with you."

After so long in solitude, Little Well couldn't help but want company. Sunrise's glistening brown eyes and long baby whiskers peered at her in mischievous fun. Little Well trickled her edge toward Sunrise and tickled her hoof. With a squeak, Sunrise danced away. All that morning, the two joyfully played until at last their laughter rang off the surrounding hills.

Maw boomed from his banks, "What right have you to offer your filthy secondhand mud to my subjects?"

Sunrise bolted from her banks in a panic. Little Well shrank even further into her hillside with a tremble.

"Your waters came from me. I gave you life, and this is how you thank me?" Maw thundered from his cataracts. "From now on, you will send all newcomers to me. When I run dry, then you may offer your waters if you dare."

Was this true? Did her waters truly come from Maw? If so, she had no right to do anything without his permission. Maw could easily flood the low plain Little Well dwelt in and drown her if he chose. From that day, she feared Maw, never again stirring her waters without a furtive glance in his direction.

Years crawled by. Sunrise grew to adulthood and brought her own young to the Valley and to Maw. Every year, she visited Little Well, who warmed a little in the young mare's friendship. Even so, scorching summers preceding snow-bitten, blighting winters took their toll upon the poor, unfortunate well until all that remained was a mere husk of what used to be. As the years wore on, it took more and more for Little Well to awaken from her long winter's sleep. All forgot her, and soon she heard neither birdsong nor cricket talk.

One very early spring day, just after the ground thawed, a disturbance at the edge of her banks brought Little Well out of her slumber. Who could that be? She awoke to find something moving around at the edge of her embankment. What could it be doing? She stirred what was left of her water. The light frost at her edges cracked and melted. Whatever it was took no notice but continued rustling about in the tall weeds that grew over her rock. Why won't they just go away and let a body sleep? Little Well bubbled a little harder and drew nearer the opening in her rock. Flowing out into the light, she came face to face with a frightful beast. It looked like a naked bear for it had no fur except on its face and head. Around its body was wrapped something the color of the sky. The something came to the tops of its bare feet and covered its arms, legs, and chest. At the waist a bright green swath went around it.

"Greetings, Little Well," the bear-creature said.

With a gasp, Little Well flew back into her cave. How did this creature know her name?

"I know you very well, little one," the creature responded to her unspoken question. "As I know every living creature in the Valley from the newest bee in the hive to the leader of the trees, Ryven the Aged, who is nearly seven thousand years old."

How could this creature know all that? No one had come to visit her for many seasons.

"I have not always been as you see me now," he said. "I have often visited you, though you've never known it was Me."

"What are you doing?" she quavered.

"Fear not, Little Well. I am only pulling the weeds away from your brim. They seem to have grown over here and choked out most of your opening. Passersby would never know there was such a lovely well here for all the weeds. There!" One last stubborn weed gave way with a shower of dirt and pebbles. "That's better, I think. Don't you?"

Little Well peeked out of her cave and looked around her brim. The freshly tilled earth quickly turned to mud everywhere her waters touched. She saw nothing but broken-down walls and naked banks. Trembling, she withdrew into the embankment.

"Can't you see it, Little Well?" the creature asked with an earnest expression. "How beautiful it will look when the spring flowers grace it. What a wonderful place to come and rest."

Something in this bizarre creature's words made her burn inside. How she longed to be open to the breezes once more. How she missed the birds and looking up into the azure face of the sky. She peeked out once more at the bear-creature.

"Not a bear, Little Well. A man. You may call me Traveller though I am Lord of all you see. That and much more. For many years, I have been tending the Valley, but now I have come to see what can be done for you. Will you not say hello at least?"

Little Well cautiously bubbled her way toward Traveller's hand.

"Greetings," he said with a soft chuckle as he dabbled his fingers in her water.

So many seasons had passed since any had been near her. She caressed the man's fingers, delighting in even the smallest companionship. Wherever He touched the algae, it fell away as if burnt. Who was this Man?

"There is much to do here if I am to help you reach your

true potential," Traveller said. "I can help you, but you shall have to trust me. Will you?"

Oh, how her heart longed to see the sky again, to feel the warm summer breeze, to be in the land of the living.

She hesitated.

The hope that had begun to blossom in her shrank back against the arctic blast of her fear. What could she do to help change herself? She couldn't even pull her own weeds or make her waters clean again. How could this Man-creature possibly help her?

"It has been a long time, hasn't it?" he asked in a voice gentle to her sorrowing ears. "Too long, in fact. Come to Me. I can take away your emptiness and fill you with the best of waters."

At his words, Little Well shot back into her cave. What would Maw say?

"You did not come from Maw, Little Well," Traveller told her sternly. "My Father made you. Maw only thinks he is capable of creating. He will shortly have to reckon with me regarding his prideful heart."

"But he says we're both made of water, which must mean I come from him."

"Your similarity still does not make him your Creator. All living things have water in them and each and every one comes from only One, My Father. He made all, and He has sent Me to tend them. Your waters are full of the dirt of envy and fear and their taste is tainted by pride. What have they gotten you?"

Still, she hesitated. Could she trust him?

"My time here is limited, Little Well. You must decide soon, for I do not know how many more times I will pass by here."

Her emptiness grew more than she could endure. Anything had to be better than this living death she suffered day after day. Traveller had been kind and taken away her weeds and tilled her hardened banks. How wonderful it felt to stretch once more. One look into His kind, dark eyes and she reached out her silt-filled waters toward Him until they touched his roughened fingertips.

"Please help me," she pleaded in a low voice. Her surface shook with grief and desperation.

He smiled and laid his palm on her waters. "Be clean."

At his touch, her waters stilled and to her wonderment, the dirt and algae that had so long clogged her shallow basin fell away and disappeared with a tingle, leaving crystal clear liquid behind. She rippled her edge around in a circle, examining her banks in amazement. Not one speck of the evil in her remained. Faster and faster she went until she made small waves in her hollow. She could scarce believe it. What a miracle! She leapt up with joy.

Traveller laughed.

Little Well slowed and gazed up into His face. "Thank you."

"My pleasure."

For many days afterwards, Gentle Traveller came and went, pulling weeds here, digging out rocks there. Wholesome grass jumped out of the ground. Wildflowers soon followed. Butterflies and bees flitted around Gentle Traveller, humming as they went about their work. They seemed to already know Him and accept Him as a friend. Little Well thrilled with each new arrival and peeked with childlike excitement as He dug around her borders too. In the ruts He planted flower bulbs.

"When will I get to see them?" Little Well asked, peering at the mounds of fresh earth. She had never had flowers so near before.

"These are narcissus. With warmth and sunshine, they should come in the summer."

"Oh."

"But they won't grow and blossom if they're not watered. That will be your task."

"Me?" She eyed the buried bulbs with anxiety.

"Yes. You must never retreat into your cave again. Everything is different now. You are a creation of the Most High, My Father, but you are also now redeemed by Me. I want you to share the life I have given you with all who come to you."

"How am I to do that?"

"Greet the morning. Sing to the breeze. Meet the animals. Tell them about Me. Above all, remain pure no matter what. That is why I have given you the flowers. Every time you water them, it helps to keep your banks clean. Every movement will help to keep envy and fear away. As for your pride, remember I am always with you, no matter what happens, and without Me, you can do nothing. That fact means everything."

Day after day brought change and growth to Little Well. Never had she known such wondrous care and companionship. She thrilled to her very depths every time she heard Him coming. Then, one day, Traveller came to Little Well, staff in hand.

"My work is finished here," He told her. "I must leave."

"Where are you going?" she asked, sorrow filling her.

He laid His hand upon her anxiously trembling waters. "I will return someday. Until then, remember all you have learned and remain pure."

"Please stay. Who will take care of me?"

"Don't you remember? I am with you always. You may not always recognize Me for Who I am, but I'll be there. I am easily found, if you look. I must go now. Peace to you, Little

Well."

In the twinkling of a raindrop, Traveller had gone. Little Well cried out to Him, but He did not return. How her heart ached! What was she to do now? She circled her banks mourning, remembering every sweet memory of Traveller. At last, the sun set for the day, and Little Well fell into a sad slumber filled with dreams and thoughts of Traveller.

The next morning dawned clear and bright, the clouds above little more than wisps across the azure sky. The next day dawned the same and then the next and the next. Still no sign of Traveller. Surely, he would return soon. A month went by. She did not move much, and her banks began to turn murky again. Fear and doubt began to creep in once more. Was it all a dream? She could hear Maw in the distance roaring his boasts to the Valley and his clamoring made her shudder.

Little Well fought against the despair that threatened to overtake her. She had almost pulled back into her cave when she remembered, *Every living thing comes from only One, My Father.* Traveller's words. She flowed out of her cave and gazed up at the pastel hues of the early evening sky.

"I don't want to be dead anymore," she told the clouds. They looked back at her passively, but between their gossamer folds she could see a tiny twinkle of a star like the gleam of a kindly eye.

"I want to live," she informed the air around her.

Keep your waters clean…and pure.

She rippled her waters in determination. Some of the scum on her surface dissipated. She rippled them again, harder this time. More disappeared. Slowly at first and then with increasing speed, she began to race around her basin, each pass sending more and more of her dirt away until her surface sparkled clear once more. With an effort, she peeped over her new embankment. As she trickled back down, something in the earth caught her attention. She drew near. What could that be? There in the moist brown dirt lay one neat footprint.

"I didn't dream it after all!" she shouted. "Look well, O sky! Bird and creature hear me. See? Gentle Traveller has given me life and behold, He left behind His mark that I may be comforted! Oh, come and see!"

Robin Redbreast hopped down from his tree and peered at the footprint, cocking his intelligent head this way and that in a curious fashion. In a flash, he flew back to his branch and burst forth into the most glorious song Little Well had ever heard. One by one, the startled birds around Robin joined in his singing until the whole hollow rang with heavenly music. Cricket added his buzzing descant to their harmony as the evening at last drew to a close.

Little Well leapt out of her basin in sheer joy, splashing

the flower bulbs and laughing as she went. With a sigh, she settled down into her banks to watch the sable folds of night descend upon the Valley. Stars winked out of their lofty abyss like gems. She drifted into the most peaceful rest she had ever known, just as the silvery moon rose over her.

"I am my Beloved's, and He is mine," she hummed to herself.

The End

"For God so loved the world, that He gave His only begotten Son, that whosoever believes on Him should not perish, but have everlasting life."

John 3:16

UP FROM THE DUST

God's Love Covers All

<u>Log Date: 025,10,2345 | Time Stamp: 01.47 | Morning</u>

I loved her from the moment I laid eyes on her. Bitai the Hermit said the name given to her by our people was *Iyani*. She was a fair skinned outsider with a smooth forehead, slender frame, and skin white as milk. Our dark, thick set, armor clad Undarii warriors laughed at her from over their wine cups, rubbing knuckles to ridged foreheads in an open display of distaste, but she stood straight and tall without a shred of fear in her pale green eyes. Her long, loose red-brown hair shone even in the smoky half-darkness of the eating hall. My heart gave a great bound when Bitai introduced her to the heads of the houses of the clans present that evening. She acknowledged each with such dignity that even our elders were impressed. I was so captivated I could hardly keep my grip on the sonic pipe cleaner I was operating.

Iyani. The name meant shining blade. Her bearing did not fit the name. Rather it be *Tok'met* or *Ingal*, two sweetly heady blossoms that were as rare as they were beautiful. No one knew exactly what planet or solar system she came from, only that she had been found unconscious on our moon base *Mihai* with nothing more than the clothes on her back and a holy book in her hand. Miracles seemed to follow her. Few, if any, outsiders ever managed to master even the rudiments of Undarii, but Iyani… She learned our language without the aid of the subcutaneous translators. Her soft voice graced the words when she spoke them and to me, she was like a holy oracle. In addition, she worshiped a single deity the same as the Undarii. We soon learned the deity in her holy book matched ours, the Great Maker.

Reclusive, silent old Bitai told the clans she was part of the fulfillment of our greatest, most ancient prophecy in which the Great Maker promised to deliver us and lead us into truth and freedom from slavery. Of course, the warriors were skeptical at first, some claiming the prophecy spoke of an Undarii, not an outsider, but Bitai remained adamant. The Great Maker had spoken. So it was written. So it would be done. The Hermit was known for his truth telling, and the elders listened.

Though she never tried to impress or brag, Iyani had a gift for engendering trust. Our female warriors especially avoided her at first, seeing her as weak, for she never picked up a weapon or drank with the men. In addition, they knew her newly exalted position entitled her to much wealth and influence. They expected her to be like them and to treat others as beneath her, but Iyani treated all as equals and the younger warriors, male and female alike, quickly drew near her table in loyalty.

"She is *mudryy*," they said eagerly among themselves. Wise. I agreed. She spoke even to me, the *sh'c roc*, a pariah and worthy of death.

"*Q'r ish toshmic*?" was her very first question to me and her soft tones well-nigh undid me. I could not have met her gaze had it been commanded of me. What was my name indeed! Praise the Great Maker, I did not stutter, though for a brief moment I felt as if a wild beast had sliced me in two. The ionic deck scrubber in my hand trembled slightly, and I rubbed my palms on my knees.

"Please, stand up," she said.

I stood, focusing my gaze to the immediate right of her delicate, tiny white foot. It was not webbed like our feet were. Neither were her slender hands.

"Have you a name?" she asked, gently laughing at my long silence.

"I am Dugal, my lady," I managed at last.

"Of what house?"

My whole body jerked with the force of that question, so much so, that at first, I could not reply. She could not know. Surely, she could not know. I did not want to think that she would ask such a question out of anything more than simple ignorance of my father's treachery and my sisters' merciless betrayal of our own family. She could not know of the subsequent seizure by the High Council of our titles, rank, glory, honor, all the things an Undarii holds dear. I set my teeth, squared my shoulders, and stared straight ahead of me as I answered. "I have no house."

I expected her to mock and turn away from me in disgust or worse, to look upon me with pity, but she did neither. Instead, she nodded somberly. "Nor do I."

Her open admission shocked me! Undarii do not speak of such things. Not since the execution of my family twenty long years ago had I said a word to anyone of the shame and pain inside me. Sometimes, I thought both would suffocate me.

"My people want nothing to do with me," she went on. "They abandoned me here on Undar and refuse to acknowledge my existence."

Everything in me ached for her, yet when I glanced at her face, I saw neither hate nor bitterness reflected there as I had often seen reflected in my own. Only sadness gathered around her eyes. I broke servants' protocol for the first time and looked into her face. How did she come to know such peace? I immediately looked away.

"You have us, my lady," I assured her. "We are your people now, and you are ours."

"Yes. So I am." She turned to leave. The sorrow in her voice touched me.

"My lady?"

She paused. “Yes?”

“Your presence is much needed here.” I stopped, my chest tight. “And wanted.”

Iyani’s face split into the first real smile I had seen since her arrival. “Thank you, Dugal.”

END DATA TRANSMISSION

Log Date: 026,10,2345 | Time Stamp: 00.31 | Morning

War with our inveterate foe, the Buildars, did not suffer Iyani to remain close for long. Bitai took her along with K'ric, M'hel, and the rest of our best warriors to the military training grounds in the *Hiktii* desert. I would not see her again for months. I missed her sorely and feared for her. I prayed genuinely to the Great Maker for the first time in years, not for myself, for I did not consider myself worthy of the Maker's notice. No, instead I prayed for Iyani. *Keep her safe, Great One!* What could Bitai possibly want with her there? She would be better off here in the mountains, among our pools and fortresses where she would be protected! She was never far from my thoughts and dreams and prayers.

Life seemed dull and empty without her nearby. I went about my duties with a heavy heart. I had to force myself to focus on the shelves I had been commanded to stock, the decks I had been told to scrub, and the isolated berths and rooms I had been given to empty and scour. I had never felt so lonely and forsaken.

Then, without warning, the warriors returned. Iyani, however, was not with them. I attacked Bitai as he disembarked from the last shuttle, strafing him with questions.

"Where is she?" I demanded, ready to choke him with the cords of his monk's tunic. "What have they done to her?"

Bitai regarded me with a bland expression when I at last drew breath. "The Great Maker forgives, Dugal," he said enigmatically and moved to one side of the embarkation ramp.

I scowled up the ramp behind him, and there she stood, alive and well. Better than well! Gone was the stranger she had once been to my people. She stood in the open hatch of the shuttle arrayed after the fashion of one of our queens and prophetesses, her long, formal robes of sepia and gold wafting around her like a mist. I could hardly breathe. The Great Maker had heard me. *Me*! Less than the least of all my people. My heart soared with hope. I knelt and touched my forehead to the ground in reverence.

"The Great Maker says implicitly," she said to me by way of greeting, "that a child is not to suffer for the crimes of the father, nor the father for the crimes of the child. He also speaks of homage due only to Himself."

I remained where I was, hardly able to hear for the blood pounding in my ears. The sacred words of our Great Maker washed over me. How I longed for the Maker's forgiveness, longed to be free of the shame my past had brought on me! Forgiveness was a foreign concept to the Undarii, particularly to one such as me. If my own people could not forgive me, how could I forgive myself? The hope that had begun to blossom in me vanished like steam in the scorching sun.

"The Great Maker is great in mercy," Iyani continued. "How can we be anything less? Rise, Dugal. Worship only him."

I blinked and glanced up at Bitai, afraid to look at Iyani.

"Do you believe in the Great Maker, my son?" he asked.

Every part of me shook. I remembered how the Great Maker had heard my prayers for Iyani. Perhaps… Silence clung to me for an agonizing moment, and I realized my only hope for redemption hung on the one who made me. What my people thought, what my lady did, or even what Bitai said, couldn't help or change anything. Only the Great Maker could free me from my guilt and shame.

"I believe. What must I do?"

"Repent, and the Great Maker will make you clean."

In the depths of my very being I sought mercy from my maker for the first time. I could think of no other words than a simple, heart-felt plea:

"Help me!"

Bitai's gnarled hand touched my head in benediction. "Rise," he commanded.

I lifted my head and rose to my feet. The Hermit's eyes lit with holy fire, and he motioned with his staff. K'ric and

M'hel stepped around Iyani on the ramp above me, one holding a pulse rifle and the other a suit of armor. What was happening? I stared in confusion first at them, then at Bitai, but I was not dreaming. I was the *sh'c roc* no more.

At first, I could scarce believe the change in my life. I entered military training for the first time in two decades. The Great Maker brought back skills I thought long lost, and I was continually surprised at my reawakening abilities. I was included in battle plans. K'ric, First Commander of our space flight forces, led me with other warriors out into battle, and I found myself sharing in the spoils.

The change in me was not just outward, but inward as well. I slept the sleep of the innocent. The shame of things my family and I had done in the past no longer haunted me. My normally hot temper and quick-for-offense nature were being tempered with self-control. I learned the difference between defense and taking offense. Bitai was like a father to me. I leaned heavily upon his knowledge of our Holy Oracles and through him and them I learned the truth of the Great Maker.

And Iyani…of course, I could not help but love her with every fiber of my being. Heaven was to be in her presence. Joy was to hear her voice, still so soft, but firm in the Great Maker's strength now, too. How I longed for her. To take her home to me. To make her my mate. She fast consumed my thoughts with a mead stronger than our most intoxicating wine. I went into battle with her name in my heart and had the Great Maker called me to the afterlife, I would have died with her name on my lips.

END DATA TRANSMISSION

Log Date: 027,10,2345 | Time Stamp: 00.58 | Morning

I was not without opposition in my newfound promotion. Like a simmering cauldron, tensions and long kept grudges frothed just under the surface around me. Few openly protested, but the resistance could be felt at the councils, from the elders and guardsmen in particular. All went well until First Commander K'ric disappeared from the building where we held our war councils. My arrest was almost simultaneous, and I was ruthlessly interrogated. My quarters, ship, locker, and belongings were scoured. A thorough search of the grounds and surrounding buildings was made. Scouts went out. Thirteen planets in four solar systems were searched to no avail. Three major battles with Buildar were thwarted in as many weeks. The war ground to a halt.

The First Commander was gone, and we had a spy in our midst. But who? I had been grudgingly acquitted, but the question remained, and still I was followed. Tracked. Listened to. Dogged. Three times, I was attacked on the streets by rioters. Six grueling weeks passed before the culprit was found: a fellow Undarii in the pay of the hated Buildarin race. M'hel, now our acting commander, and his squadron questioned him for days. Much information was discovered, but not K'ric's whereabouts. Nothing more could be done.

The traitor was hanged, and war resumed. Our vigilance tripled. War councils moved from place to place, never meeting in the same location twice, but nothing seemed to have changed. Our efforts continued to be thwarted. Battle after battle continued to be lost. Thousands upon thousands died. All Undarii outposts and settlements retreated to our home planet in an agony of terror. Suspicion grew like dust canker on metal. Rumors flew. Chaos reigned.

To my surprised delight, Iyani turned to me in her anxiety over K'ric and the progress of the war, pouring out her frustrations and feelings to me. She had truly taken us to her heart and saw us as her own people. I sought Bitai and the Great Maker for wisdom to share with her. We prayed together. She joined us in the search for our commander. I was appointed as her bodyguard. I did not, however, give a second thought to the Hermit's words shortly after the First Commander's disappearance.

"Undarii mate for life. One love for always. Two hearts joined and beating as one."

Eight months went by and though few others than me noticed it, Iyani's chest began to pain her. Several times, I saw her gripping the railing of our flagship as if in the throes of some tremendous battle. Her knuckles turned white with the intensity of her grasp. Perspiration broke out upon her brow. The sight of her growing suffering made me anxious. I prayed unceasingly to the Great Maker for her, hoping fervently that she would regain her health, but when she collapsed during a war council, I could no longer deny facts. I carried her to our ship's SickBay and laid her unconscious in a bunk.

Bitai's words came back to me like a death knell: "Two hearts joined and beating as one." K'ric and Iyani were mates. The longer he remained prisoner, the harder it would be for her. Every battle he fought, she waged with him. Every torture or pain he endured, she shared. Neither could fight two wars at once. If K'ric was not found soon, Iyani would die and with her the hope she had come to symbolize for our people.

The realization struck me so hard that I could not breathe. My whole being shook as I struggled from SickBay to find Bitai. He did not reproach me as I poured out my anguish to him. I had known. I had *always* known the truth and my friend and champion had tried his best to warn me, to spare me. My sense of loss was impossible to measure. I thought I would die right there in the Hermit's quarters. I staggered out into the passageway, pulling at the collar of my uniform in a futile effort to inhale. My chest heaved with an unutterable pain. In my suffering, I vaguely remember Bitai gripping my shoulder in a vain attempt at comfort as I clung to the bulkhead. I shrugged him off with a feral cry and stumbled to my quarters where I unleashed my rage.

I didn't have much in my quarters, but what I had, I destroyed. Glass and pottery shattered against the bulkheads. I tore my clothes, pulled my bedding to shreds, and pounded the deck with my fists. When at last my strength was spent, I sank to my knees, threw back my head, and roared my pain to the stars. The rest of the night, I spent alternately cursing myself and beseeching the Maker to either give me Iyani or take my life. I loved her. I could not live without her.

I spent the last three days in my quarters, chronicling my brief existence. I neither ate nor slept. I opened the door to no one, not even Bitai, who I am sure has spent the last hour trying to get in.

Iyani loves K'ric. Not me.

The desolation I feel right now has stripped me of all desire to even live…

END DATA TRANSMISSION

The truth stares me in the face for the first time, and for the first time, I can face it even though it sears my heart every time I see the words in my log: "*Iyani loves K'ric. Not me.*" The last year has been incredible. I thought dishonor and servitude would be my lot forever when my father and sisters died for their treachery, and I had been punished for my own. But the Great Maker saw fit to lift my head out of the dust and make me one of his own people.

I raise my head. The Great Maker chose me as one of his people. The meaning of those words come ringing home to me as clearly as the peal of a temple bell. If I am one of his people, I must obey him. Did not the Holy Oracles state that true love put others before oneself? If I truly love Iyani, I will put her desires and wishes above my own. My beloved needs me. My people need me. I am here for such a time as this. Why do I sit here idle while she and the one she loves suffers? I must do what I know I must. I take a deep breath and lean forward to tap two controls on my computer console.

WristCom | Date: 027.10.2345 | Time Stamp: 07:00 | Morning

Something drips on my foot. I look down and realize the side of my left fist is bleeding. I examine my hands and realize my attack on the deck of my quarters has left both hands a bloody pulp. I rise from my chair and cast a brief glance at my computer. The last three journal entries have vanished from it like a beautiful, elusive dream. I know in my heart the Great Maker is behind me and before me and has placed his hand upon me. Instead of the gut-wrenching pain I have been feeling for three days, I am at peace. I turn away completely to tend my hands with a skin-knitter.

There is no time to tell anyone the plan that is forming in my mind. I strap on a long side knife and slip a shorter boot knife into its sheath. Then I simply walk out of my quarters to the hangar deck where our fighter pods and flyers are held. Few are in the hangar other than a deck lieutenant and a maintenance chief. I make sure they do not see me stow a travel pack, extra helmet, MedKit, and pulse rifle in the side compartments of a twin engine fighter pod we call an Assassin. I chew my lip. Will I need food? I decide to travel light. If food is needed, I will hunt.

Next, I openly climb into a flight suit and tell the deck lieutenant I am going out for a routine flyover. He checks my

ID card. Someone else was on the docket for the flyover. I tell the lieutenant he is in SickBay, and because of my rank he permits me to proceed. Despite my military training, my conscience bothers me at the blatant lie, and I beg the Maker's forgiveness as I climb into the cockpit. I flick switches and press buttons to taxi out onto the runway, then I take off in a roar of engines without once looking back on my homeland. If the Great Maker wills it, I will one day return with our First Commander. If not…I do not allow myself to contemplate that possibility.

Once out into deep space, I initialize the Assassin's cloaking shield and head for the shadow of the nearest uninhabited moon where I can view the interrogation files I brought with me. I hope they can give me some clue as to K'ric's location. I watch for several hours. The spy was well trained and knew how to resist our methods of information seeking. As the interrogation progresses, Commander M'hel asks the spy where he had been on a particular date.

"*Mnboa*," he replies.

My ears prick up. Most Undarii would not know that name. Indeed, Commander M'hel passes over it without notice, but with my own family's background in treachery, I know it at once. Mnboa is an insignificant Buildarin outpost in the northern hemisphere of the planet *Set* in the *KahRen* System. Well-hidden, and deep in the moist forests the

Buildarins so much prefer, it could be a prime place to take a prisoner of war for torture. It will be as good a place as any to start.

Set is two light jumps away from the Undarii home world, a day's journey if I'm undetected. I set the coordinates and less than twenty-four hours later, I am staring down at a dark green globe hanging in the night sky. The planet Set is so unlike our glorious golden sand swept hills and deep-set sapphire pools. The sun here seems cold and distant.

My console beeps a soft tone, and the vid-screen initializes. I lean forward, scowling in concentration and feel my eyes widen in surprise at what I am seeing. Gone is the tiny outpost that used to be there. In its place is a full-fledged fort complete with a powerful satellite and tracking device. A satellite of that size could easily keep watch over the comings and goings of the KahRen, *Eel Tahk*, and *Guhl* Systems combined with all their planets and ships. I sink back into my seat. *No wonder we've been losing the war!*

I check for weapons and defensive technology. At first, they seem wholly unprepared for attack. Minimal armaments. Two fighter pods and a small contingent of guards to keep watch over the living quarters and a narrow compound surrounding the thin spire of the central guard tower and satellite. That can't be right. The vid-screen beeps again and I realize why they are so minimally armed. Inverted vapor fencing keeps anyone or anything without a neutralizer band from breaching the perimeter from the inside. Getting in will be the easy part. Getting out will take an act of the Maker.

I activate the pod's cloaking shield and ease the Assassin down on an open ledge surrounded by trees on the northern slope of a mountain ridge closest to the fort. From my vantage point, I look down and tap the vision enhancers built into the lenses of my helmet for a closer view. Eight Buildarin guards are billeted there, their tall, lean reptilian bodies sheathed in sable and green bio-armor that fits like a second skin. Two Buildarins stand on the eastern side. Four are in the tower. The presence of two guards at the living quarters indicates they are holding something or someone there.

I go back to the pod for my pulse rifle and then head down through towering trees, fallen logs, and massive boulders to the fort. Twilight is fast approaching, and a thick fog is settling as I make my way downhill. I know I will be able to do nothing until the next dawn after I have had a chance to rest and observe the comings and goings, but I want to be as near the fort as possible lest I miss anything at all. I shiver as I bed down among the underbrush and damp moss at the base of the shield, my rifle resting in my arms. Moisture drips off the leaves. Silence wraps around me. The last thing I hear before drifting into sleep is drunken laughter.

WristCom | Date: 029.10.2345 | Time Stamp: 05:30 | Morning

I am awakened by the sounds of orders barking from frog-like throats. I check my wrist communicator for the time and my eyes move in the direction of the sound. My helmet allows me to see the living quarters. The guard is changing. Mealtime. Small talk. They move about their routines. Guards in the tower walk back and forth watching the sky and their equipment. When the sun is just over the trees, I hear a deep thrumming sound coming from the tower. The satellite has been activated! I wonder what battle is being thwarted today. How many Undarii will die? My blood boils at the thought, but my heart sinks, too. It will take more than a fighter pod to destroy that satellite from the air.

The whine of engines draws my attention skyward. A lean sliver of a ship lands point first among the trees like a dagger. It would appear by the insignia that an officer is arriving. I tense and shift in my place quietly. The ship lifts off with near silent grace, leaving the officer and his attaché standing in utter silence in the center of the landing field. The officer strips off his gloves and surveys all around him before moving. Together the two stride forward and the vapor fencing ripples as they step onto the main compound. The two guards outside the living quarters snap to attention.

Though little is said, it is obvious the officer makes the guards nervous. His arrival is imposing…and unexpected. It takes him and his companion the rest of the morning to inspect the satellite and surrounding area. Everyone is anxious to please, slithering hither and yon, bringing touchpads and computers for them to view. I glance upward through the mist. The sun must be mid-sky by now. A commotion yanks my attention back to the enemy below.

All but the guards in the satellite have gathered below in the compound and are at attention. At a signal from the officer, two guards enter the building and in a few moments they all but drag a sagging figure out by the arms. Together they secure the prisoner's wrist restraints to a post in the middle of the open compound, forcing him to a standing position. The attaché is seated at a small table, evidently taking notes. I curse the planet whose sun will not shine enough to burn away the mist for me to see clearly. As I try to determine who the prisoner might be or from what planet, the officer pulls from his belt a short, thick, benign looking handled cord that belies its true malicious purpose. My hand tightens on my rifle in dread. I have seen one of those before.

The officer approaches the prisoner and speaks to him. The prisoner returns no reply. Again, the officer speaks, but to no avail. For an hour this pantomime goes on until at last, the officer grows tired of mere talk. He shakes his wrist and the flexible cord bursts out into a sickly shade of grayish-orange glow. A cruel smile spreads across the reptilian face, and he says a final word before swinging the cord across the prisoner's body. The helpless man arches away from the pain, but there is no escaping it. I can hardly bear to watch! I cannot hear any sound, but I can see the terrible effects of the electrostatic cord. Burns crisscross the prisoner's back, arms, and legs. The officer stabs the prisoner with it. His skin bubbles and blisters.

Sickened, I draw as near to the perimeter of the fencing as I dare. I squint at the prisoner. He has dark, coarse hair and suddenly, my skin prickles in rage. Through the welts on his back and the glimpses I can get of his chest, I see the trademark tan and sepia skin whorls of a fellow Undarii! I lean forward but cannot see his face. I do not know who he is. After what seems like an eternity, the officer throws his cord down in disgust and stalks into the living quarters. The guards are dismissed. The attaché gathers his things. I shake with wrath! I want to tear the filthy bog crawlers apart with my bare hands! No one deserves such treatment.

Time ticks by, and the officer returns outside, wiping his face from having eaten. I grind my teeth, struggling for breath. He snaps his fingers, and the attaché scurries over to pick up the cord and hand it to him. He intends to continue his torture. My stomach turns over. I cannot endure watching another session of this evil. I must move while everyone is distracted, or I will not be able to do anything. Whoever this Undarii may be, I cannot leave him to die like an animal. I pull back into the brush and make my way behind the living quarters. To minimize the pulse in the shield, I crawl through the fencing on my stomach into the shadow of the barrack's generator and await darkness. I wish I could have waited outside the fencing. Anguished screams and the harsh Buildarin tongue echo off the stone walls. I am forced to listen … and beseech the Maker for mercy.

Twilight at last begins to fall and with it silence. Relief floods me. A light illuminates the small window above where I crouch. I hear a group enter the quarters. The sounds of eating and drinking reach me, but I hear no speech so the officer must be with them. At last, I hear talking. My translator picks up bits of different conversations, but most are too soft to be heard clearly. The front door opens and then slams shut. The light goes out, and all I hear is the thrum of the satellite and the guards on duty.

WristCom | Date: 029,10,2345 | Time Stamp:11:59 | Night

I wait thirty tics more before I make my move. The guards in the quarters will be the easiest to deal with and will not be expecting anything. The officer and tower guards will be a different matter. Then what to do about the satellite? Signaling for a ship would take too long and would attract the attention of Buildarin warships. How do I destroy this thing? If I could get the shield down, I could destroy it with my fighter, but what about the other Undarii? The prisoner would be in no condition to help with the shield. He might be able to destroy the satellite and fly off the planet in time to avoid the explosion, but I wasn't sure. I chew my lip in frustration.

The darkness in this accursed forest is deep, but I am used to the cavernous blackness of Undar. Even without my vision enhancers, I can see perfectly. Knife drawn, I enter the barracks with the stealth of *d'hajo*, Killer Shadow. I bare my teeth. Four well placed thrusts silence the guards forever. A final stroke of my knife puts an end to the pathetic little attaché in his makeshift cot in the corner. At the back of the narrow room is an arsenal. Ion rifles. Shock rockets. Ah! Neutralizer bands. I rip two from their case and retreat as silently as I came.

The prisoner is still tied in the compound, sagging limp against the restraints. My hand is on the door when I see the officer come down from the tower. I freeze and then melt into the shadows. He barks an order from outside. He barks the order again, louder. When he receives no reply, he bursts in, bellowing. Before he can touch the lights, I am behind him with one hand over his mouth and the other pinning his arms down.

"Death to all tyrants!" I snarl in his ear and wrench his neck sideways.

He does not have time to cry out or even breathe. I let go of the body as I would a diseased corpse. I stare down at him in fury and hate as I hurry to pull on his uniform. I may only have moments before the other guards come to investigate the officer's sudden silence. Even though I am broader than the Buildarin, his bio-armor molds to my form as though it were made for me. I look around as I pull on his cap. Behind me is a storage closet. I press the body into it, close the door, and exit the barracks as calmly as I can. As I pull the barrack door shut, something collides with it with a soft clink. I look down, and there is the infamous torture cord. I pick it up with shaking hands and hang it reluctantly from my belt.

Pulling the cap down over my eyes, I keep as much to the shadows as possible and make my way to the base of the satellite. Once there I ignite the cord and slip it into the control panel. Boots clang overhead. I freeze. But it is only the guard walking his normal route. I close and lock the panel and then move back into the shadows the way I came. A search light sweeps the compound.

I make my way back to the prisoner. With my back to the control tower, I face him and grab his hair as though I am interrogating him. His shoulder muscle twitches, and his blood-caked head lolls to one side. I let go of his hair in shock.

"Commander K'ric!" I hiss, shaking him. "Commander!"

He moans something unintelligible through swollen lips. I glance around. The compound darkens as the light sweeps past nearby.

"Iyani," he mumbles.

Pain shoots through me at the sound of her beloved name. My hands shake as I search for the release on his restraints. They unlock at last, and he sags to the ground with another moan. I snap a neutralizer band on his wrist and another on my own and then pull him up and into the shadows. The clock is ticking.

"We have to go, Commander," I whisper in his ear.

Grasping his belt, I pull his arm around my neck and all but drag him through the fencing. I struggle up the first of several steep inclines into the darkness, taking most of his weight. He stumbles, and I strain against him trying to steady us both. We almost go down completely. I lose my footing in the wet leaves beneath me when a webbed hand grabs me by the throat. I am thrown against a tree, my own knife at my throat.

"Who are you?" K'ric snarls. "And what is your business with me?"

Fighting my surprise and lack of air, I manage, "It is I. Dugal!"

"The *sh'c roc*?" he sneers.

I try to nod and cannot. "The satellite…" I croak.

"What of it?"

"It's…explode…"

K'ric's hand tightens on my windpipe. "You lie! You are here to challenge my claim to Iyani. She is *my* mate. If you've harmed her…"

I pull down on his hand and rasp out in equal fury, "I could never harm her! She is my heart, but it is you she loves! Not me. It is you she lives for, no matter how much she has done for me and our people. Her heart beats with yours. Your pain is hers. Four days ago, she collapsed, and I know it is because of your absence."

K'ric slowly lets loose of my neck. As I suck in air, I notice his eyes get a faraway look in them. I look away. Such a love comes only once to an Undarii, and I can hardly bear to see it, knowing it can never be mine.

"Is it so?" he asks.

I draw in a ragged breath. "It is."

"Why should I believe you, *sh'c roc*?" he spits at me. His eyes take in the Buildarin uniform I am wearing.

I laugh bitterly, all my noble reasons for coming momentarily forgotten.

"If I wanted you dead, Commander, I would not have risked my life to bring you this far. I could easily have made it look as if you'd died a prisoner of war." My teeth clench in anger. "Or worse. I could have left you in that courtyard to die slowly at the hands of the Buildars. Isn't that what you'd expect from my family? But there isn't time. That satellite is rigged to explode, and Iyani will die if you do not return. I came to save her and our people."

K'ric glares at me for a moment. As if to punctuate my point, a growing rumble starts to build below us. He gestures with the knife.

"Lead on then."

I go.

WristCom | Date: 030,10,2345 | Time Stamp: UNK | Early Morning

We almost reach the clearing where the pod is hidden when shouts ring out below us. Our escape is known. Buildars are swift climbers, and our time is rapidly running out. The rumble from the satellite is growing to a roar.

"Quickly!" I urge and glance back. Fire from the satellite is licking upward, lighting the sky like a furnace. I turn to the commander. His face is a sickly shade of white.

"We cannot risk hand-to-hand combat," he wheezes as he comes alongside me, clutching his sides and swaying. Sweat pours down his face. For all his bravado, I know he's battling pain and losing. "We must reach the pod before they find us."

I stop.

He eyes me with open mistrust and my patience evaporates.

"You think I don't know this? Bio-armor can withstand several direct shots from a pulse rifle at close range. We will never make it if you do not let me help you. Now, give me your arm!"

K'ric grinds his teeth but slings his heavy arm over my neck, matching his feet to my stride.

"The pod is just over that ridge," I tell him and pull him

along.

We barely reach the pod's hatch when an ion pulse shrieks past me, lighting the pre-dawn air with a bluish white glow. Brush and leaves rain down on us. The cloaking shield hums as the shot ricochets off it. Gritting my teeth, I deactivate the shield and all but throw the commander inside, leaping after him and pounding the controls to seal the hatch.

I scramble into the pilot's chair, punching controls before I'm fully seated. The pod lurches into the air with a roar, rocking and pitching. I manage to switch from cloak to defensive shield, but only after I lose three antennae and a small communications array. Tree limbs fizzle upon contact. Ion pulses continue to pummel the pod even after we're in the air. A tremendous clap of thunder explodes in front of us as a shock rocket narrowly misses its target. The pod lurches to one side with the blast. I fight the controls to right her. At last, the pod gains enough altitude to initiate a light jump. The flight's bumpy this low in the atmosphere, but I have no choice. Before we make the jump, I make sure to strafe the fighters and flaming debris that was the satellite before it blows completely.

Once in space, I switch back to the cloaking shield and push the Assassin's engines as hard as I dare. I must get back to Undar with the information and the commander. My inboard computer blips an ETA.

"We'll be back on Undar in twenty hours, Commander," I say.

When I get no reply, I glance over my shoulder. K'ric is passed out on the deck of the pod, his chest rising and falling in much needed sleep. Relieved, I turn back to check my instruments. Twenty hours. Twenty hours until what? The past days' events have gone by in such a blur, I have not had the chance to consider what I would do when I found the commander, if I ever did. Now I'm faced with the awful prospect of going home to watch the lady of my heart love another. I know I can never love anyone but Iyani. She will no longer need a bodyguard. To return to my post is unthinkable. I must go, but where?

Lost in thought, I lose track of time. When I shift in my seat a searing pain shoots up my ribcage and down my left leg. I grab my side with a hiss. The vid-screen blurs in front of my eyes. I shake my head and look down. Blinking dizzily, I take my hand away from my side. It is covered in my own blood. What? I shake my head again, trying to clear the buzzing in my ears. It's a fight to keep my eyes open. I blink again. A voice shrills in my ear and my eyes fly open. What? Who? Someone is calling out something.

"Landing coordinates...correct your course...attention! Attention!!"

My body twitches, and a cry escapes me. A powerful

arm reaches past me to tap the computer console. I blink once more.

Darkness closes around me like a long tunnel.

Disembodied hands remove my helmet and pull on my arms. I'm floating upward. The hands push me down on something hard and flat. I want to scream. Instead, I gnash my teeth. A soft beeping echoes in the background. I feel myself moving. My head swirls around with the unknown voices around me.

"It's the commander!"

"K'ric!"

"Contusions. Lacerations. Burns. Here you! See to this one!"

My eyelids are pried open. Lights flash in my eyes. I cringe away from the pain in my head.

"Pupils sluggish. Ion blast to the side."

"Get him to MedCenter One. Move! 40cc's…"

The beeping in the background continues. I hear calls for medicines. Bandages. Sedatives. Then…

Darkness.

"Dugal?"

Who calls? I struggle upward through the darkness that is holding me down. My mind turns into a swirling mess of thoughts. Flowers. Bandages. Buildars. Forts. Explosions.

Bright lights. My eyes flutter. Blink. Blink. Pain!

"Dugal!"

Iyani! My heart leaps and the sudden surge of blood makes me dizzy. I hiss and cough at the same time. White and green spots of pain burst behind my eyelids.

Consciousness begins to slip from me. My eyes and mouth won't work. *Oh, Holy Maker, help me! Let...me...see! Please let me see her!* My eyes flutter open at last, and her lovely face comes into focus above me.

"Oh," I exhale in wonder. I drink in the sight of her creamy white face. Curling red-gold hair. Pale green eyes, like two pools of the purest water. Some of that water drips from her chin onto my face as she takes my hand and holds it to her cheek. She is crying, something Undarii cannot do. Iyani's blood people do so for loved ones. My heart nearly breaks.

"He is dying," someone nearby whispers.

Iyani's face crumples and more water flows from her eyes. Dying? Panic rises within me like a flood. No! K'ric cannot die! With a mighty effort, I drag air into my lungs and whisper her name.

"Shh, my friend," she soothes, laying a finger on my lips and smoothing my cheek. "Save your strength."

I try to shake my head. Strength is fast leaving me. My head leans into her hand. Her forehead is so soft on mine.

"C-commander?" I slur the word and grit my teeth with a soft growl of frustration. *Oh, Great Maker! Don't let me have failed, I beg you!*

Iyani lifts her head and looks over her shoulder. K'ric's troubled face comes into view above me. He lives! Relieved beyond expression, my eyes roam Iyani's gentle face. Bitai approaches my bedside. I am so tired. I can barely hear what he says. I can hardly keep my eyes open.

"The prophecy is fulfilled, my son," he repeats.

I take a deep breath and turn my eyes to look up at him.

He smiles down at me and lays a hand upon my shoulder.

"The Maker foretold it and today, because of you, the fate of Buildar is sealed. Honor is restored to your family. Undar is saved. Well done."

My heart soars. The Maker has made a place for me among his people and among my own at last! I can scarcely believe it. K'ric and Iyani will live and prosper. So too will my people. *I praise you, Most Holy Maker, for your wonderful works to me!* A full smile spreads over my face and peace floats down over me like a blanket. I rest content under its warmth. The last of my strength ebbs at last and, unafraid now, I let go. My eyes flutter and then close, and I am too weary to open them again. The voices around me grow more and more distant. A light in the distance, like a far-off sunrise, grows brighter and brighter.

"Forgive me," is the last thing I hear.

It is K'ric.

The End

"Humble yourselves therefore under the mighty hand of God, that He might exalt you in due time: casting all your care upon Him, for He careth for you."

I Peter 5:6-7

ADDICTION, THE APOSTLE PAUL, & ME

An Autobiography

God's Love is For Everyone Who Believes

I think we, as Christians, sometimes do each other a disservice to a certain extent when we share our testimonies. We try to "one-up" each other, as if we have to make God look good or sound better or as if God couldn't save anything less than a mass murderer or a drug addict or an alcoholic. Don't get me wrong. God "is no respecter of persons," meaning He doesn't discriminate. Rich, poor, high, low, it doesn't matter. He sent "His only begotten Son that *whosoever* believes in Him should not perish but have everlasting life."

God has plucked some people out of great sin, and it shows His great power and glory and love! And I'm not saying we shouldn't talk about it, but what of those who have lived normal, everyday lives? Is God's power and glory any less glorious or powerful? Am I any less worthy of God's "attention" than a convert from a Muslim country because I was born in a Christian environment? Certainly not. As the Scripture says, "all have sinned and come short of the glory of God." Ultimately, our testimony is not about our back story, but the fact that God has redeemed us from our sin and made us free. Free from sin. Free from slavery. "And whom the Son has set free, is free indeed". The details leading up to and surrounding our individual stories of freedom are just that: details. However, the main character is God.

My life story before Christ is a normal one. I had the privilege of having both parents around. I had schooling at home, church, and in a public setting. I had a home, a brother, pets, clothing, toys, and food. I was even in church nine months before I was born. In some ways, I feel a little like the Apostle Paul in the Scriptures, "of the stock of Israel … a Hebrew of the Hebrews … a Pharisee …" And before you ask, no, I'm not Jewish, but I definitely grew up religious. I taught Sunday School and kids' clubs for a long time. I also did a lot of volunteer work, and I loved it. I wasn't consciously doing it to earn my way to heaven so much as it was the "thing to do.'' Oh yes, I was religious, but I was empty and dark inside. And I knew I was far from perfect.

I could, and did, blame my temper and unforgiving, vengeful spirit on my ancestors. I tried to blame my rage and malicious, hateful speech on the bullying I got particularly in public school. And that was just a short list of what the Scriptures called my sins. But when I was finally able to be completely honest with myself, I knew those things, those sins, were coming out of me and no one else and no matter what I did, I could not get away from them. Camp revivals and memorizing Bible verses and praying and witnessing didn't change who I was inside. Promising myself I'd be a better person didn't do anything either. I was filthy with not only my sins, but also the works I was using to try to erase them.

I started wanting to change at the age of twelve after seeing a movie relating the story of the courage and peace of a persecuted Christian in China. I couldn't put into words what she had, but whatever it was, I wanted it. And in typical stubborn me-centered style, I set about to get it. It took me ten years to realize I couldn't get rid of the darkness, the sin, inside me. I began to discover that all those "works" I'd done and was still doing were my futile attempt to fill a void inside me.

Ten years of fighting to be good, praying, repenting, weeping, working, striving passed until at last, at yet another community mission work, I was spent. Of course, it helped that I'd been sick with the flu after working for two months straight, seven days a week, fourteen hours a day, but as God says, "all things work together for good to them that love God, *to them who are the called according to His purpose.*" Around midnight on October 31, 2002, I remember struggling under the weight of all my sin and the futility of all I'd spent my life doing to be shed of it. I prayed that night, "Jesus, help me!" and at once, I fell into the most profound restful sleep I think I've ever had. The next day, one of the first thoughts to go through my mind was, *There's light in my house*! And for me, that was extraordinary, because for the first time, I didn't have that weight on my heart that I'd had all my life, that darkness. Just like an addict or an alcoholic whom God has delivered, I too was delivered from the shackles of sin and hell. And trust me, to be without God no matter whether you're drunk or sober is still hell.

Satan was on the outside for the first time that day. He no longer had control of me, and he still doesn't. I no longer *have* to do his bidding. I can say no. Why? Because I'm God's child. God is my Daddy, and it is through His authority that I stand. Jesus is my big Brother, and it is because He died for me that I can stand in victory over sin. And they'll help me and do help me. Through Christ, I forgive, because God for Christ's sake forgave me. Through Christ I have control over my mouth, and I continue to put away wicked things because God loved me enough to cleanse me. It's a path. A way of life. I am no longer the person I once was. Now I'm "a new creature" being made into Christ's image.

Do I fall off the wagon? Yes. Because like the alcoholic or addict, I am not perfect. I want to go back to what's easy, what's familiar, what's tempting, what's comfortable. Letting go of my old life has been and still is a little frightening. I sometimes forget that I don't have to earn my Heavenly Father's love. I forget I am called to be holy and apart from sin. When I forget, some of the old darkness comes back. I take a good shot of the old life, and I get good and sick on it. Then God reminds me, gently, that I have His love already and nothing can separate me from it. Jesus has paid it all. I'm still His child. He will always forgive me. Through Him, I can do all things. He will always love me, and nothing will ever make Him stop loving me.

I am secure.

"If the Son therefore shall make you free,
ye shall be free indeed."
John 8:36

ABOUT THE AUTHOR

An avid reader of all types of literature, Erina Sinclair has had a love affair with fantasy and fiction ever since she sat at the table listening to her mother read great authors like Tolkien, MacDonald, Milne, & Lewis aloud over lunch. She believes books are a welcome escape from a crazy world, but more importantly they are a chance to learn, too, in a setting more easily understood than in a textbook or lecture.

Her passion is weaving stories with parable-like meanings and painting pictures with words that show God's love, power, and truth. Erina lives with her beloved husband where they enjoy long walks, playing practical jokes on each other, and going to the beach together.

Connect with Erina online:

Facebook: www.facebook.com/Erina Sinclair22

TWITTER: @ErinaSinclair

Thank you

for reading our books!

Look for other books

published by

TMPbooks

www.TMPbooks.com

If you enjoyed this book

please remember to leave a review!

Made in the USA
Columbia, SC
30 October 2022

70155685R00083